PREFACE

In a world where power is born in the eyes and destiny is determined by colour, *The eyes of the wicked* follows the journey of a boy who began with nothing — no power, no name, and no hope. What began as a wish to die slowly turned into a will to protect, to rise, and to discover not just who he was, but what he was meant to become.

This story was written with the belief that strength doesn't always come from being the most powerful — sometimes it comes from enduring, from refusing to give up, from protecting those you love, and from daring to change the course of fate.

As you read the chapters ahead, you'll walk alongside Emmanual Godson, a boy burdened with tragedy and gifted with extraordinary potential. You'll watch him grow, fight, fall, and rise again in a magical world where eye colour defines everything — identity, strength, and even one's place in society.

This book is for the dreamers, the outcasts, and the fighters — for those who have felt powerless and dared to believe they were meant for something more.

Welcome to *the eyes of the wicked*.

THE EYES OF THE WICKED

Volume. 1

Ch 1 – *As lucky as Lot from bible*

"Why am I this lucky", says a person whose family died, the only person left alive but badly injured was his father. "At this point I am willing to die". This person was not so happy with his life, he was so unhappy that he wished he could die, just like his family died.

In this world where power was everything, there were many wars to gain power and it was not just any war it was a magical war since everyone had different magical powers based on their eye colour. There were four different eye colours that gave different powers, they were, red, which helped in manipulating time, blue which changed position of things, green which can read minds and change thoughts, and yellow which can be used to copy any other eye's ability except the green one. Out of this green was the rarest one.

He hated his life so much that he lost his will to live and even forgot his name!

He used to call himself Lot because he lost his parents in a war but he was not killed because the enemies did not kill him and he was left at the brink of death by his own friend. His friend's father was a part of the enemy army who killed his family except for him and his father, they were not killed because of their good relations with his friend's father, or so they thought, they were badly injured. Lot was 3 years old during this incident, and was very traumatized. Now that Lot was 9, he wanted to die but he was unable to. He tried drinking poison so many times that his body was now immune to them. He tried falling off from high place but got saved many times. He tried cutting his veins but he was saved by the locals of the village he lived in.

His father was injured so bad on the neck that he had permanent loss of speech and he could not even move because his limbs were cut off, so he had to stay at home and could not even help his son to do anything. Even though his condition was that bad Lot cared so much for his father. He did everything he could to help his father, he saved money to buy his father artificial limbs that could have helped his father walk again but that money was stolen by burglars.

"Dad, I promise I will become the eye king and give you a better life" says the boy, with tears in his eyes.

The eye king was the most prestigious post a person can obtain and the eye king was chosen by God himself; he was the strongest person alive.

"Dad I am 9 right now that means my eyes will awaken next year" says Lot, eyes awakened once the person was 10 years old and based on the eye colour the people were sorted into different schools, the schools were 'The red school of time', 'The blue school of position', 'The green school of minds', and 'The yellow school of copying'.

The life of Lot and his father was full of hardships for the next few months, Lot used to work at different places to get enough money for next year so he can get into one of those schools.

A few months later he had enough money for his eye awakening. He went to the Palace of eyes and applied for his eye awakening. The eye awakening ceremony was a very famous ceremony where the whole country got excited. Now Lot just had to wait a few months before he could awaken his eyes. He was eagerly waiting for the ceremony because he wanted to get into the green school of minds and become the eye king to help his father.

He wanted to give his father the life he dreamt of and wanted to fulfil all his dreams, though his dream of becoming the Eye king might or might not come he wanted to try.

Ch 2- *The Awakening*

After waiting a few months Lot was ready to go for the Eye Awakening Ceremony. He was very excited and wanted to go to the green school of minds because he wanted to know what others thought of him.

The next day Lot reached the Palace of Eyes and bumped into someone he thought he did not know, "sorry, I didn't mean to" says Lot to the man. "Oh, it is fine, wait, you look similar to someone I know" says the other boy to Lot. "Let us be friends then, what is your name?" asks Lot, "you can call me Louis Sato, my name might be weird because I am Anglo Japanese" says louis. "Oh ok, nice to meet you…" says Lot. Lot and Louis exchange their phone numbers and are interrupted by the announcer "Ladies and Gentlemen, as y'all can see over here we have got a good number of children participating in the ceremony over here, so brace yourselves because this year I can sense a good amount of Eather from the students"

"What is Eather?" asks Lot to Louis, "I don't know, probably the power you release from your eyes" says louis. "Oh okay" says Lot. The announcer announces "May all the children listen over here, line up for your awakening".

All the children run up to form a line, and are asked to drink a potion that makes a change in their eye colour, and based on their eye colour they are sorted into different schools. After waiting an

hour in line, it was Louis's turn to drink the potion, he drinks the potion and his eye turns into a bright red

colour. Louis gets really happy because that is what he wished for. He is now taken into the red school of time.

Next up in line was Lot, he stepped up and drank the potion waited a few minutes but nothing happened, he thought that his eyes will awaken in a few hours, he waited and waited but nothing happened.

He was really sad because he cannot become the eye king without any eye colour, his eyes were brown in colour which signified no power. He thought he will have to work as a slave because the people with no power in their eyes are supposed to work as slaves. Even though his father had yellow eyes he could not use them because of his loss of speech in the battle of power, so his father could not chant spells.

The next day he received a notice from the eye palace saying they have to shift to the slavery district by next week since neither him nor his father can use magic. Lot read the notice and burst into tears he did not know how to tell it to his father, so he just kept the notice aside and decided to leave the country and hide in another country.

He started packing everything that they might need in this journey like food and clothes, he told his father that they are leaving because there are many thieves in this country. After packing everything they needed they were about to sleep until one of the biggest criminals, named night wizard entered his house and asked for all the money he had.

Lot held a knife in his hand to fend of the criminal, the criminal had a brown eye colour as well so Lot was at an advantage, until the criminal ran towards Lot's father and held him as hostage. This was a huge problem since Lot had to save the money he had for his journey to another country.

"Drop the knife right now or maybe you won't be able to see your father a few minutes later" said night wizard, which was true since he committed countless murders just like that.

Night wizard was at a huge advantage until..., Lot's right eye shined bright blue like a gem of sapphire and he released such a high amount of Eather that the criminal was blown away he changed the position of the criminal using his eye magic, he bought the criminal close to him and held his neck so tight that it destroyed the windpipe of the criminal.

Lot's left eye got blood red and just the Eather released was enough to kill the criminal. Night wizard's head burst into 20 pieces.

"Oh man I wanted to cut it in half" said Lot covered in blood.

The next he goes to the palace and shows the eye examiner his eye colour. "that's some rare eyes right over there, two different eye colours huh, you are a strong boy, you better keep those eyes safe" says the examiner, "definitely will keep them safe, and I don't have to be a slave now, right?" asks Lot. "Yes, you don't have to be a slave now. And since you have 2 eye colours you can choose which school you want to go in, red or blue?". "Oh ok, I want to go to the red school of time" says Lot. He gets happy since he is in the same school as Louis.

Lot was very excited to go to school he went home to tell his father about that and now that they will not leave the country, they had to unpack all the things they packed, that was a work that took time since they packed almost everything.

Two different eye colours was a pretty rare thing since only a few people in the country had that and they were considered gifted directly by God himself. Things were looking really good for Lot.

Though Lot was very happy he wanted to go into the green school of minds and wished he could make everyone think good about him, but now that he had two different eye colours everyone thought good about him already.

Though one of his wishes was fulfilled, his other wish of becoming Eye king was still far from complete and he was very determined to do that.

Ch 3- school supplies

The school announces about a meeting which all the first-year students are required to attend. So, the next day, all the students gather at the school. The students wonder why they were called and discuss to find the reason.

"Good day children, it's nice to see you all gathered over here. Children, you can call me Erin, I am your teacher and hope you have a fun time about manipulating time. And students please gather near the dining table we are going to have a feast."

Lot feels happy about getting into the red school because the teachers seem really nice. He tries to search for Louis but he does not find him.

After the feast professor Erin gives each of the students a list of items they need to buy, the list varies from student to student based on their Eather level.

The next day near a shop Lot meets Louis. "Hi, long time no see" says Lot, "indeed" says louis.

Lot tells Louis that he got in the red school as well and they both talk about going to eat together sometime.

Lot asks "where were you yesterday? and why didn't you come to the gathering?", "I couldn't come because my car broke down and by the time we fixed It the gathering was over and I couldn't attend the feast, but I was just in time to get this list"

"By the way how many items did the school ask you to purchase from this shop? I got 22" says Lot. Louis freaks out and says "22!! Mine says only 6, I think that is a bit too much". "Got any idea where an iris cooler is and what it does?" asks Lot, "um no, let's ask one of the adults in the shop, but why do I not have it on my list?" says louis.

Both of them buy the items they need, reach home and start packing the things they are going to need in the school since it was starting from tomorrow.

Ch 4- the organization

The next day Lot goes to school and meets louis, both of them greet each other and try to find the way to their classroom.

Lot had a really bad feeling of something bad that was about to happen, he thought louis was acting a bit weird and that made Lot suspicious.

"How are your parents doing?" asks Lot, "they are doing good, in fact they want to meet you, so do you want to come to my place?" says Louis. Lot says "Yes, sure, but when?", "maybe today at 5, if you are free" says louis.

Lot agrees and reaches home eats lunch and feeds his father as well, and books a ride to Louis's place. He reaches the area where louis lives in and sees huge buildings and offices.

 Louis was from a rich family and has a huge house, and Lot did not know about that so he gets confused and enters the wrong house, that is where he finds Louis tied up on a chain shouting for help.

He sees a huge door on which he knocks, waits some time and the door does not open, he knocks again and this time the door opens, he sees 20 people sitting next to a chair on which someone is tied up using ropes. He realizes that the person on the chair looks similar to louis.

"Is that louis?" asks Lot to the kidnappers, "indeed is, want to join him kid" says the kidnapper. "Nah I am good but you won't be good in a few minutes" says Lot with his right eye shining blue and his left eye shining red. "I see, you are strong enough to stand my presence" says Lot impressed by the kidnappers.

"What do you mean strong enough, you are weak kid" says one of the kidnappers.

"Well then I will put my powers to the test" Lot says. "Try and save your friend if you can kid" says the kidnapper. "ha-ha I already did, look who I have in my hands right now" says Lot with louis in his hands "That's an illusion, turn around idiot" said the kidnapper pointing towards the chair with his green eye shining.

"Oh man, you have the eye I always wished for" says Lot, "keep dreaming idiot, now I will defeat you with the eyes you wished for."

Lot appears behind one of the criminals and uses his blue eyes to change the position of the brain of the criminal and removes it out of his body. He uses the red eye's abilities to make the brain decrease in size as it becomes younger.

He proceeds killing all the criminals and saves louis. Louis says "you sure you are 10 years old, show me your birth certificate, because that was a slaughter." "I am 10 years old like look at my height I am 4'2 that is 5 inches below average" says Lot. Louis thanks Lot and says that he was here since the last 5 days.

"5 days! no wonder you were acting a bit different at school, that must have been a clone. I will drop you till your place."

They reach louis's place and his parents thank Lot and invite him for dinner. Lot being fond of food accepts and eats a lot.

Louis's parents ask him stay at their place for a night because it was dark outside and Lot accepts because he left a caretaker at home for his dad.

The next day Lot and Louis reach school and they are surrounded by hundreds of children asking if they can take a picture with Lot, he does not understand what is going on and then they are surrounded by news reporters asking Lot how he defeated 20 people at once. Lot being an introvert, fainted. Louis had to carry him to class.

Everyone started taking a liking towards louis and he started making many friends. He was loved by everyone in his class. He loved his friends and wanted to become strong enough to protect them with all his might.

Ch 5- the mountain of Yomigami

After a few days the school announces a field trip to Japan, and everyone gets excited since all of them have different reasons for going to Japan, some like Japanese cars and some like anime so everyone is very excited.

"I wish I could meet Eiichero Oda and sir Toriyama" says one of the students, "me too I am a big fan" says another classmate.

"Children start packing your bags we are leaving for Japan on 27th February 2024 and we will be reaching on 1st march in Kyoto" says professor Erin.

Lot was a sword critic and was very excited to see the different swords in Japan he liked katanas a lot and wanted to buy one from Japan.

They are told that this was a hiking trip and they are staying in hotel at a valley between mountain Yamagami and mountain Yomigami. Mountain Yomigami was a forbidden mountain because of its past, there was a war that happened in there and there were many casualties.

They reached the hotel and slept through the night. The next morning, they had to go to climb the mountain Yamagami, which was quite easy for Lot because it was not so high and very short compared to mountain Yomigami.

Lot wanted to climb mountain Yomigami so he tried going near it but was stopped by professor Erin. Lot was bored and asked louis what he was doing. Louis was crying and told Lot about the death of Akira Toriyama, he was a great writer and louis always wanted to meet him. "He will always be in our hearts and we will miss him" says louis with a tear running down his eye. All the people who liked Akira Toriyama were crying and wished they could do something about it using their eye powers but using eye magic to bring someone back to life was a crime and the Government had placed magic barriers so no one could do something like that.

Lot could not see his friends crying and wished he could do something so he wondered that if he climbed the forbidden mountain will there be something that could increase his power tremendously and he could do something about the deaths of people and bring them back to life.

The next day when no one was looking he went towards the forbidden mountain to climb to the top of it. He saw many signs which said that the mountain was forbidden and that he should not climb it but he ignored all of them and was halfway done with climbing the mountain. He was already above the clouds and was catching his breath.

He kept going despite the lack of oxygen determined to reach the top. After climbing for a bit more he was almost there, the sky turned black though it was morning he could hear the sound made by the ravens he heard a faint but demonic voice that said "Go away, you aren't worthy" he felt that someone was watching him. He turns around and sees a sword.

Being a sword critic, he goes near the sword to unsheathe it but is stopped by a person that just appeared out of thin air. "Don't unsheathe that sword or you might die" says the person. "Who are you? and how will I die if I unsheathe the sword?" asks Lot. "I am Seiran, I protect this sword so no one unsheathes it and dies, anyone who is not pure and merciful enough can't handle the cruelty of the sword and dies. Did you hear a voice when you came here?" says the person. "Yes, I did hear a voice asking me to go away when I came here, it was faint and demonic" says Lot. "You might be able to unsheathe it soon kid just be kind and merciful enough to people you love" says seiran.

Lot runs away from there because he was not able breath, and goes back to the hotel and sleeps without telling anyone what happened.

The next day is their flight back to their school and Lot still did not tell anyone what happened on the mountain and keeps it to himself. They reach their school and everything continues like normal.

Lot does what seiran asked him to do, he tries to become even more kind and merciful.

The next month it was the last day of school before summer holidays, everyone is excited, since it was the last day of school everyone thought of partying and bought different types of snacks and were having fun.

But Lot was still wondering what he saw and he was curious about what will happen if he does unsheathe it. He wanted to learn about the

legend of that sword and wanted to learn more
about it.

Ch 6- the island

Lot's summer holidays begin and he decides to take his father to an island. He did not have money at first but then he remembered about the need based financial aid program launched by the government in which he can get money based on work he has done for the country and since he defeated 20 criminals, he got enough money to take his father to the Yakobi island.

Yakobi island was a very tropical island and had many mountains, and was a very good place for a vacation. He booked the tickets and did not tell his father about it since he wanted to surprise him.

The Yakobi islands was not just famous for mountains it was also famous for their knowledge about swords, and Lot wanted to know more about the sword on that mountain so he decided he will visit the library of Yakobi to know more about that sword.

They pack their and are ready to leave for Yakobi islands after a few days, Lot is very excited because he wants to learn about the sword on the forbidden mountain and his father is excited as well because he did not travel for 4 years.

A few days later they reach they island check into their five-star hotel that Lot bought with the money he earned by defeating the 20 criminals, he was happy that he was able to give his father a luxurious life.

Lot asks about the sword to the locals but they refuse and don't tell him about it. Then he just decides to find it out himself. He goes to the Library of the Yakobi islands and searches for 4 days straight and he finds nothing about the sword so he decides to leave but then he remembers that one of his friends that he met in the school gathering had green eyes which will help him read the minds of the locals.

He uses his blue eyes to bring his friend Nick and he reads the minds of the locals but he can't tell Lot about it.

He then went back to the hotel and beside his room was an old man's room, he was quite helpful and did not believe in curses and told Lot about the sword.

He said that other locals were not able to help him because there was a curse on the sword that whoever spoke about the sword died in an unusual way in a few days.

He can finally enjoy the sceneries in his hotel room; he could not do that before because he spent all his time in the libraries trying to know more about the sword.

Ch 7- the Noble duo

When Lot came back from the islands of Yakobi he had to do his holiday homework and get ready for school again.

After a few days his school reopens he meets louis again and they talk about what they did in their vacations, and then Louis tells Lot about their exams that are around the corner they only have a month to prepare.

Lot ignores it and continues to not concentrate in studies; he thinks he can finish the whole syllabus in one night and does not study at all.

Studies go on as normal and Lot does not concentrate at all though louis and his other friends ask him to.

The next month his exams start and he has to study all night but does not understand anything, he wishes that he would have studied before. "I wish I could read minds" says Lot worried about the exams.

He tries reading a few more hours but he still does not understand anything. The next day he goes to school without learning anything, he goes to the exam hall, sits on a chair, picks up his pen and starts writing whatever comes to his mind, and he does not realize it but his eye shines green, as bright as an emerald.

Nobody else sees it.

After writing the exam he goes home and while changing his clothes he looks into the mirror, and sees that some part of his right eye is shining green while the rest is shining blue.

He goes to the palace of eyes and asks the eye analyst about his eyes.

"What are those eyes? Never saw those wait I will ask my higher-ups" says the eye analyst.

He asks his higher-ups and they freak out, "so the prophecy was real, it has come true"

The higher-ups say "what prophecy, tell me "Says the eye analyst.

The higher-ups say "here read this book" handing a book called the prophecies said by the king

The analyst reads it and says "no way, it is on the first page" he does not believe what is written and looks at Lot's eye and realizes that it matches what's written in the book.

"Wait let me see" says Lot snatching away the book,

he sees nothing in the book and says "what? There is nothing written, what are you all talking about". "So, the prophecy is true it says the person with three eye powers cannot read it, the person with three eyes was just said to be a myth for the last 100 years. Take this kid in custody we are examining his body." Says the analyst calling his guards.

The guards take him to the lab for examining and hand him over to the scientist. "I see, you have interesting powers" says the scientist. The scientist asks him to stand in the cube of examining.

Lot stands there and the scientist starts examining, he does that for a few minutes but it does not work he tries again but this time the system crashes and says that his body is too complex to examine. He gets no information about his three eye colours even after trying for hours.

 "Wait, no way kid what is your last name?" asks the scientist, "umm, I don't know I forgot." Says Lot. "What do you mean you forgot? You have noble Eather in your eyes; you are the second noble family in our country the first one is the Sato family so try to have good relations with them" says the scientist.

Lot thinks "Sato, I might have heard of that name before". "Wait so I will get like money for just existing because I am a noble" Lot says to the scientist.

"Yes, in fact you can go to top schools and use the best facilities that the government will provide" says the scientist.

Lot reaches home and sees a notice from the government on the table which says that he will be given a new house and he got a new bank account with lots of money and he is asked to join the top schools.

He does not understand what are top schools and just ignores that.

The next day he goes to school and asks Louis what are top schools.

"Top schools? Um those are schools which nobles attend, you can't attend those, and I can but I don't want to" says Louis, "you are a noble as well?"

Asks Lot.

 "As well? Of course, I told you right I am of the Sato family" says Louis.

"Oh yeah I forgot to tell you I got my body examined yesterday and turns out I have noble Eather in my eyes, so I am a part of a noble family somehow and so is my father." Says Lot

"That means you also got house from the government, so it is in the same area as mine what is your house number?" asks Louis "oh that, my house number I forgot but I think it was 17107" says Lot.

"17107! That is right beside my house" says Louis.

Both of them are happy now because they can be together more often and become better friends.

"let's come to school together every day so that we can become better friends, and let us study together more often, I am bad at studies" says Lot to louis, "yeah sure let us go to school together every day, and what do you mean you are bad at studies, you got pretty good grade, in fact you got more than I did" says Louis.

"Oh, my marks, um, don't tell it to anyone but I have a third eye colour, so right now I have the powers of blue, red, and green eye colours" says Lot. "Oh, I get it now, you just read someone's mind and copied their answers, no wonder you got good marks.

I thought you worked hard it." Says louis, "eh no working hard for exams is for nerds, I definitely won't work hard for exams anytime soon" says Lot. "I agree bro, I just got good marks and did not even have to work that hard, like compared to others who pulled all-nighters I got pretty good grades." Louis says bragging about his academic excellence.

They talk sometime and louis invites Lot and his father to a Noble family feast next week. Lot accepts and tells his father about it.

The next week they enjoy the feast, it also made their relations with the other noble family better.

They reach home and see another notice saying that they have been offered a full recovery of their body that recovers all their injuries, Lot and his father get really happy since Lot will finally be able to listen to his father's voice again and his father will be able to walk again.

Ch 8- The name

The next day Lot and his father reach the noble recovery station and they are given a potion, the doctors in the station say "that potion recovers every injury in your body and makes your body as good as it was before getting the injuries, so drink up". They drink the potion and nothing much changes about Lot but his father completely changes and all the scars on his face vanishes his legs start appearing out of thin air and he stands up and was so happy that he hugs Lot, he realizes his voice is back and he could finally speak he clears his throat and says "son, your real name is......" he clears his throat again and says "Emmanual, Emmanual Godson is your real name son, and thanks for the recovery son, I love you, and you probably forgot my name as well it's Wilbur, remember it" after hearing Emmanual cries and hugs his dad tight.

"I love you too dad, you are the best" says Lot. They go home and talk about what happened when Emmanual was little, he does not remember anything that happened back then and asked his father many questions.

"You are definitely not like me, I did not ask these many questions when I was a kid, you are a rather curious one, that was the quality I wish I had back then just like you do, I could have been a way better dad, I don't even remember everything about your childhood" says Emmanual's father.

Ch 9- The tournament of Schools

The next day Emmanual and his father were watching news of a killer who escaped prison, they say that the killer always wears a white hoodie, he asks his dad about him. Even his dad knows nothing about the killer.

He goes to school and tells Louis and others about his real name and that his dad has completely heal. Louis says "oh that's perfect for the tournament coming up, prepare well, we have to win this time, the red school has not won for three years", "there is a tournament? I didn't know about that, but we sure will win, because we have me." Says Emmanual with a smirk on his face. "Bro stop bragging, I know you are strong, but there is a strong guy from the yellow school which might be hard to defeat, no one ever saw his face because he always wears a black hoodie" says Louis. "I will be able to defeat him, trust me" Emmanual says. "Well, he will try to target you because you are the strongest, stay safe" louis says.

During lunch he meets that person and they talk for a bit but he was not interested in talking more. He poisons the drink that Emmanual was about to drink.

Emmanual drinks it but nothing happens he just continues talking to louis and that person in the hoodie is shocked.

"So, I will have to defeat him by myself" says the person in the black hoodie.

 For the next few days all of the students practice their fighting skills to win the tournament and make their schools proud.

He tries so hard to awaken all his eyes at once again but that required to much energy and he could hold that state for a few minutes and he wants to win the tournament.

He wants to make his father proud and win the tournament. He tries holding that state for longer every day and the longest he held that stage was for 26 minutes and 47 seconds. He trains longer and longer every day because he did not want to lose.

After a few days the tournament begins and the number of audiences overwhelms all the students they are under a lot of pressure and all of them are determined to win the tournament.

The tournament starts and Louis is supposed to fight in the first round against a student from the yellow school, but the yellow school had a trick up their sleeve all of them copied Emmanual's abilities.

"Look, I know you are going to lose so I will explain you our abilities so you can stand a chance next year, our abilities are basically gambling we copy others abilities and the accuracy of the copied abilities from 1% to 99% percent are completely luck based, hope you understood, now take this" says a person from the yellow school who tries to teleport behind Louis and punch him on the neck.

"I see you are quite fast; you will need to be faster to defeat me, I know you copied Emmanual so I am quite familiar with his abilities" says Louis.

"We will see about that" says the person from the yellow school with his eye shining bright blue

He teleports behind him again and leaves a decoy there so when louis turns back, he could punch him on the chest to paralyze him, so he could kick him any times.

Louis saw through it and caught him by the neck to punch him, but then his other eye shines red and he reverts backs time to go back to his original position.

"You are a tough nut to crack huh" says the guy from the yellow school.

He immediately fasts forward time to go back to the place where he placed the decoy and this time lands a hit on Louis's chest; louis starts bleeding and falls to the ground.

The doctors come to take louis away and cure his injuries. Emmanual sees this and a few rounds later it was his turn to fight, but there was a lot of pressure on him since if he lost red school will be eliminated, so he definitely had to win this one for the school and it was not looking good for him, he was up against the strongest person from the yellow school.

The round start and they talk for a bit and Emmanual realizes that only one of his eyes is shining yellow, he sees that his other eye does not even emit light.

Now he gets curious but he does not have time to think as a punch comes straight towards his face which he dodges with ease and moves back, he is not even able to read his mind because it was too dark.

His curiosity gets higher and higher every minute so he ghost steps gets behind his opponent and tries to remove his hoodie but fails, he tries again and again but fails all the time.

"I see, you want to see my face, here feast your eyes on the black eye I copied a few months ago, be sure to see all you want because you won't be able to see them again" says the person from the yellow school revealing his black eye which releases so much Eather that Emmanual is flung a few hundred meters away, and starts bleeding.

"Those are some nice eyes you have right there, guess there is no point in holding back anymore, right?" Emmanual with his eye shining in three different colours.

"You too have some nice eyes" says his opponent while charging towards him, Emmanual dodges and hits him with a spear followed by a number of punches which he dodges.

Emmanual teleports behind him and hits a hook kick which makes him bleed from his head so the match is a win for Emmanual but he sees something no one else saw.

Emmanual saw that his opponent injured himself to stop fighting no one knew why.

He goes to the yellow school's locker room where he tries to find him but he was not there.

He sees a bag which was kept on the bench near the locker of the person who he defeated and checks the bag to see if there is any contact information of that person, but instead he sees a white hoodie with some blood stains.

He remembers that hoodie which he saw on the news, and he realizes that his opponent was the under-cover killer. He informs the cops and the school board about it and all of them try to find him.

The tournament is postponed since one of the students went missing, and Emmanual was happy that his school qualified for the finals but he was still curious about that student he fought in the tournament.

After a few days they find him and arrest him since he killed many people. Emmanual goes to the prison where he is kept and asks the people there if he can meet him.

They allow him and he goes in to talk to him. "So long nerd" he says to Emmanual. "Indeed, now tell me why you lost on purpose?" Emmanual asks him, he says "none of your business, I am impressed you noticed though, good job". Emmanual asks many times but he refuses to tell. Emmanual thinks "I see, my visit to the prison was not so helpful, I am still curious though".

Ch 10-How school got better

Professor Erin stood at the front of the classroom, a wide smile spreading across his face as he surveyed the sea of eager young faces looking back at him. The anticipation in the room was palpable as he prepared to unveil an exciting announcement. With a theatrical flourish, he clapped his hands together to capture everyone's attention. "Children, brace yourselves! We just got a new subject added to our curriculum, and I can hardly contain my excitement! Now, I want you all to take a wild guess. What do you think it is? Anyone...?"

"It is.... Swordsmanship, so I request everyone to buy a sword from the school supply room and start practicing" Emmanual and Louis go to the supplies room to buy one and Emmanual freaks out since he did not know that the school had such good swords.

"Yo Louis look isn't it exquisite.... The curvature is honest, the kissaki crisp and resolute. You can tell this blade this blade was not just crafted; it was breathed into existence. A true extension of the warrior's will. And look at this one, now that is something worthy of its lineage. The Hamon dances like smoke on still water, the grain speaks of a patient forge and the balance- it's like holding purpose itself" says Emmanual, "did not understand a single word of that, just pick a good sword for me"

"Fine here take this it's really good" says Emmanual handing a katana similar to what he took and Louis takes it.

They go home and give their parents the consent forms they got from the school about the new subject, swordsmanship.

They agree and tell them about the rules and regulations about using a sword, and turns out Louis's and Emmanual's dad were pretty good swordsmen back then, it was quite nostalgic for them.

The next few days they start learning about swordsmanship and the history of different types of swords, but Emmanual he just did not get the right feeling from his, he always wanted one of the best swords and wanted to use them.

The next few days of using that sword, he was not able to bring out his full potential in that sword, he felt a strange feeling when using that sword and did not like it.

That night he heard a strange voice saying "come unsheathe me quickly". He recognised that voice and realized it was the one he heard from the sword at mountain Yomigami.

He thought he was now pure enough to unsheathe it and decides to go to Japan to get that sword. He books the tickets and asks permission to the school for taking a leave.

In a few days he reaches Japan and goes to that forbidden mountain to unsheathe it, he climbs to the top again and starts having problems in breathing just like before. The sky turns black and the voice that was asking him to unsheathe the sword stops, he goes near the sword, he is stopped by Seiran. Seiran sees him again and tells him that now he was calm and merciful enough to unsheathe it. He sees the bodies of a thousand dead men; he goes towards the sword and unsheathes it.

All the bodies of the thousand men disappear and he hears the souls inside the sword screaming. Seiran is impressed and gives information about the sword he says that the name of the sword is kanshou no reikon or the wailing soul.

He tells Emmanual about the legend about the sword, the sword that has the souls of a thousand men inside it.

Emmanual decides to release the thousand souls inside the sword and free them. He does it and the souls come out of the sword he does not hear the screaming from the sword anymore.

The souls inside the sword thank him and swear their allegiance to Emmanual, they are really happy since they are finally free after a thousand years. They say that they will protect Emmanual and stay with him forever.

Emmanual keeps that sword with him and decides to use it in school as well instead of the sword he took from the supplies room.

He reaches his country again and when he goes to school next day everyone are shocked after seeing his obsidian blade. They ask him where he got that but he does not tell them.

He goes to the swordsmanship class and professor Erin himself gets shocked to see it and wonders how a seven-year-old is able to wield that sword.

Ch 11- The way to get stronger

The next day in class professor Erin says "now listen up children, you have to coat your sword with Eather, that is a good way to get stronger, based on your eye colour you can manipulate different things using your sword, now all of you, since you have red eyes y'all can manipulate fire using that sword, except Emmanual who also can manipulate water."

"Hah, jokes on you I also have a third eye" Emmanual whispers into Louis's ears. "Now stop bragging, I know you can" Louis says.

"Now to do that concentrate your Eather on your sword and think of the eye's ability you want to use" says Professor Erin

Everyone try to do it and all their swords light up with flames, but Emmanual is not able to do it for some reason so he asks the souls in the sword for help. They say "got you bro", they extract the Eather from his Red eye and embed it onto the sword.

"Now since we embedded the Eather for you on the sword, it will activate once you snap your fingers" say the souls in the sword.

Emmanual snaps his finger and his sword lights up as bright as the sun and Professor Erin is impressed at Emmanual.

"Great Job Emmanual, use that in the tournament once it begins again and our school will definitely win" professor Erin says while clapping his hands. "Sure, will use it professor, we will win for sure" Emmanual says, "we will have to prepare for that one, be sure to prepare the tournament is going to start again in a few days and we are in the finals against the green school" says professor Erin.

Emmanual practices everyday to infuse his Eather with the sword without using the souls trapped in the sword. He tries it so many times but fails to do it.

He keeps trying, and one day Louis sees him do that and teaches Emmanual how to do it.

"That sure will be helpful for the tournament, thanks Louis" says Emmanual thanking Louis.

Ch 12- The tournament

After a few days the tournament begins again, and there are a lot more audience than there was before, maybe because it was the finals between the green school and red school.

Another reason could be because both of the schools have acquired even greater powers and the swordsmanship of the students is beyond anyone's understanding.

The people fighting in the finals were Emmanual and Louis who were against the strongest students from the green school, it was tough for Louis and Emmanual to win.

They wanted to win because their school had not won since the last three years.

The crowd shouts louder as they wait for the fight to start, everyone is cheering for the school they support, but this time there was someone special in the crowd.

It was Louis's and Emmanual's dad sitting beside each other, the crowd are excited to see the two of the greatest swordsmen in history, the crowd got way more excited than it was before, even though the tournament did not start and there was an hour left all the seats were full.

Louis and Emmanual continued practicing and both of them were determined to win and bring a trophy to their school. It was not going to be easy though the people of the green school were formidable opponents and were quite hard to defeat. Their mastery over their eye powers was better than Louis and Emmanual, but they did not know swordsmanship.

An hour later the tournament final match starts and Louis and Emmanual are fired up since they want to win this time. The match starts with greetings from the people of the green school. It was Emmanual who had to fight first.

"You won't be able to defeat me just using your eyes you will need to use your swords, or it will be too easy for us to win" says one if their opponents, with his eye shining green and looking towards Emmanual.

"Hopefully I won't have to use one of my abilities, that will be an easy win for me, I will coat my sword with my Eather instead" Emmanual says while drawing out his sword and his eyes shining.

Emmanual uses his red eye and coats his sword with Eather. His sword shines as bright as the sun. "Oh, you learned how to do it, good job" Louis says while cheering Emmanual.

Emmanual tries attacking with his sword and tries to hit an attack infused with fire, he hits it and says "didn't know y'all are that weak, get stronger".

But then thee person he hit vanishes and he hears someone say "turn around kid that was an illusion" Emmanual turns around and sees that the person he attacked is right behind him and can easily land a hit on him.

Emmanual moves aside to not get hit by him; he then realizes that he was behind him all the time. Emmanual asks him "why didn't you attack me? you had a clear hit" he replies with "it would have been too easy then, I want the fight to last longer, you know school is getting boring, so don't hold back, understand"

"Ya I won't, what do you mean don't hold back? I want to win the tournament" Emmanual says. He then steps back as if he is charging an attack, and then looks towards his opponent with his bright red eyes shining as bright as ruby.

He then unsheathes his sword and then runs fast towards his opponent in a thrusting form. He gets closer and does a thrust, but that was a decoy and he then turns around and hits a vertical strike which scratches his opponent's head.

"Ha, got you, that was an illusion idiot" says Emmanual's opponent with a smirk on his face mocking Emmanual, "ha, so was mine" Emmanual says while slowly disappearing and appearing right behind his opponent pointing his sword toward his neck which shines so bright that it blinds his opponent.

"that's one point for the red school, students fighting in round 2 gear up and enter the stadium please" says the announcer.

Emmanual meets Louis and motivates him and says "bro you have to win this one, if you win, we will win the best of three and the tournament, imagine us lifting the cup, you have to pull this off"

Louis gets completely fired up and determined to win more than ever before, he steps up with a smile and enters the stadium, though he loses his confidence, he gains it back once he sees his father.

Louis's opponent also steps up, with unwavering confidence he says "fight well, Louis", Louis was shocked as he did not think that anyone from another school would know his name, and becomes even more confident.

The announcer says "let the battle begin" and everyone in the crowd gets excited. Louis and his opponent start the fight and greet

each other.

Louis also uses his Eather in the red eyes to coat his sword, his sword turns bright fiery red in an instant, this shows that his mastery over Eather control was higher than Emmanual.

"That was fast, the other guy took longer to do that" says his opponent impressed by Louis's master over Eather control. "Well, yeah I taught him how to do that, so it's obvious that my mastery will be higher than him" Louis says.

They begin fighting and exchange a few punches, Louis draws his sword again and then he hits a vertical slash towards all his sides, he hits his opponent but he vanishes. "Nice try, but I saw through you" says his opponent with his eye shining green.

Louis thinks "I guess I have to gamble it; I will have to combine the Eather in both of my eyes to increase the range of my sword, I will try it though I have not mastered it yet".

Both of his eyes shine red and his sword shines even brighter, he tries hitting a vertical strike the same way again but it scaled the whole stadium this time. He thought he hit him this time but his opponent disappears again and appears right beside him, catching the dull side of his katana, he punches Louis on the neck.

"Good game bro, I changed your thoughts into thinking that I was there all the time" says his opponent.

The announcer announces, "That's a win for the green school, the final round that will be tomorrow will decide who wins the tournament, it's a bit different this time around, it's a 2 versus 2"

Louis goes back to meet Emmanual, Emmanual says "it's fine, he was a formidable opponent, we will definitely win tomorrow". Louis says "in the battle just now I discovered something, I will teach It to you, it will make you stronger"

They go back home eat dinner and Louis starts teaching Emmanual, how to combine the Eather in two different eyes, Emmanual finds it difficult so he takes the help of the souls inside the sword.

Louis never saw those souls so he asks what are those, Emmanual explains him and Louis notices the three-eyed soul in the sword.

"You have the soul of a person with the powers of three eye colours, can I have it so I get stronger" Louis asks, "yeah sure you can take it, his name is Nicholas, he is a soul from a thousand years ago"

Louis thanks Emmanual and they continue practicing. After a few tries Emmanual also gets it and decides to use it in tomorrow's match.

The next day they reach school and go to the tournament, they see that today there is an even bigger crowd. Louis gets nervous seeing the crowd, Emmanual sees him and tries to calm Louis down, but then both of them see their father in the crowd and become full of confidence.

The students from the green school arrive, their unwavering confidence stays the same even after seeing such a huge crowd.

The announcer announces that the match will begin shortly and that they have a special guest about to come.

The people start discussing about who the guest could be, they wait some time and then they see a car only the king of the country owns, it was a loud car that was coming at full speed, everyone gasps and look towards the car, and they then realize that the special was the king of the country himself.

"Bro, we have to win this one, fight well" Emmanual says to Louis, "bro we will win because we practiced combining Eather and look at them, they don't even have a sword"

A few minutes they line up to enter the stadium, determined to win the tournament, the students from the green school also line up for the tournament.

They greet each other for the tournament and wish each other good luck.

They start fighting, take their stance and start exchanging punches and kicks. Emmanual gets hit by one of them but it was an illusion and he was already flying in the air, he says "Louis listen up, mix up your red eyes with the blue eyes of the soul I gave you, and make sure to mix more Eather of your red eyes, you can use it to manipulate air and fly". Louis tries it and joins Emmanual in the air.

The students of the green school are confused, but they do not have time to think about that because Emmanual is already chanting something, they get even more confused.

 Emmanual chants "Hear the cries beneath my flesh-Sorrow unshackled, anguish unbound. Let the wailing rise like thunder. Kanshou No Reikon…. ROAR for me!!" he laughs like a demon and says "I did not want to do this, but I want to win this battle, sorry Soul Echo"

He cuts his hand and covers his blade with blood and sends a devastating wave of psychic pain, it hits on of his opponents and the other one dodges. The person who was not able to dodge just fell to the ground and was not able to stand up, they had to take him out of the battle field.

Emmanual spreads out his hand and looks up to the sky and continues laughing, he then snapped his finger and teleported right behind his opponent. His landing was so tough that it left a huge crater on the ground and just that was able to lift up his opponent, he goes right behind him again, and punches him hard enough so that he falls to the ground, making another crater.

"Ha, that was an illusion idiot." His opponent says to Emmanual, "so was mine, IDIOT" replies Emmanual with his sword on his opponent's neck.

"That's a massive win for the Red school of time, congratulations" the announcer says. The team of the red school head towards the trophy.

All the teachers congratulate Emmanual and Louis on their win, and they ask them "how did you combine the Eather in two different eyes/ I didn't even teach that to you, who taught it to you?" Emmanual says "oh that, um, Louis taught me, that helped a lot in the tournament, we won because of Louis"

"Oh, great job Louis, thanks to you we won, how about we have a feast, and lift the trophy together, after all this is the first time we won in 3 years" says professor Erin to Louis, "yeah sure that will be cool, I will tell it to Emmanual as well"

Everyone is happy and are excited about the feast and are lifting the trophy and calling their family to celebrate. Even their family members are proud of their children and are offering gifts.

Louis and Emmanual meet their parents and they see them talking with each other. Louis and Emmanual are happy to see them talking so that they have better relations with the other noble family.

The next day Louis and Emmanual reach school and see that everyone lift them up and party with them.

After some time, they go to meet Professor Erin and he takes them to a 5-star hotel.

Professor Erin congratulates them on their victory again, and says that this was an important achievement that will motivate them to get stronger and grasp the essence of Eather control.

After the feast when Emmanual and Louis reach home, they see a letter. It was a rather expensive letter, which was coated with gold and had a diamond stuck on it.

They see the letter and realize it was from the King himself, the letter said that they were offered the position of a court guard. The letter also gave information on what a court guard was and the duties of a court guard. A court guard was a person who protected the country in times of war. The leader of the court guards was second-in-command to the king, and also the successor of the king in some cases.

Both Emmanual and Louis were excited since both of them wanted to be the king of the country. They happily accept and it was easy for them since the court guards worked only during times of war and just had to live a normal life when there is no war.

Now that they were court guards, they got even more famous at school, but since they got more famous more people started getting jealous as well, but a few haters were nothing compared to the number of fans they had since they were the reason the red school won the tournament.

Now that they were court guards they lived even more luxurious lives, since they were already nobles, they got money just for being in the country and got a house, and now on top of that they got money as court guards even thought there was no wars at the time. They bought different cars and tings they liked.

Their fathers were proud of them for becoming court guards and they said that they were also court guards back then, but Emmanual's father could not continue as a court guard after that war since his limbs were cut. Back then there was not a machine to analyse someone's body so they had different methods to see if someone was a noble, that did not work on Emmanual's father and he was not recognised as a noble.

Ch 13- The untold Truths

When Emmanual reached school the next day, they were announcing the results of the tournament and he saw something which reminded him of someone.

He saw the rankings and realized that the yellow school was disqualified from the tournament since one of them was a criminal. Emmanual was still curious about why his opponent from yellow school lost on purpose, so he goes to the prison where that person was.

He reaches and meets him but this time he was not wearing a hoodie, he asks him why he did that but he sees something strange, one of his eyes was black he sees that eye and he feels a weird sensation, it was like he saw a place he never saw just came in front of his eyes, it was like a completely different realm, like a realm where demons live. So, he just leaves the prison without even completing his conversation.

He wants to go there and wants to know what there is, but he could not use his blue eye to transport himself there for some reason he thought that maybe his mastery over the blue eye was not enough travel there, so he decides to go to the blue school for a month, and no one could even stop him because he also had the blue eye and was a noble.

He tells Louis about changing schools for a month but not about that realm he saw, he wants to keep it to himself and tells it to

no one.

He stays in the blue school for a month and learns how to use his blue eye more effectively and travel to farther places. His Eather in the blue eye increases and so does his mastery over water manipulation. He also learns some new techniques for battle that he could use in battle which will help him in the tournament of schools the next year.

The next day he uses it to teleport to the place he saw when he looked at his opponent from the yellow school who was currently in jail.

He reaches and feels extremely hot; he saw multiple creatures that looked way different from humans and was disgusted at their look he sees a sign made out of a very unique type of wood which did not burn even in such hot conditions.

He walks around for a bit and sees the glimpse of a devil-like creature different from all the other creatures he saw, he instantly look away since he could sense an immensely high Eather from that creature but then he hears a voice saying "leave the demon realm" and he realizes that creature told it to him. He looks at that creature once again and sees he also has black eyes. He then realizes that his opponent from the yellow school had the same eye he thinks "perhaps he copied it from that creature", he hears the same voice again and gets terrified, he instantly leaves that realm and returns to his house.

He tells it to no one except professor Erin; he asks him where he could find information about the history of eyes. Professor Erin says "I don't know about that one you will have to ask the professor of the blue school, he knows every single place in existence"

After hearing this Emmanual goes to the blue school once again to ask their professor about the place which has all the information of the history of eyes. He says "how about I take you to the library of eyes, it's a library which has all the information about eyes, it has existed for 10,000 years" Emmanual gets excited and agrees to go there.

The professor of the blue school says "oh yeah I just remembered, you studied in my school for a month and don't even know my name, it's Albert", "oh yeah neither did I tell you my name, it's Emmanual" says Emmanual.

Professor Albert uses his blue eyes to go to the library of eyes, Emmanual is amazed by how huge that library was but he does not see any book about the history of the black eyes, but he sees that his sword starts shining. He unsheathes his sword, and he sees that a bright light is emitted out of the sword pointing towards a book in the library.

 He picks up that book and hears the sound of a door opening, all the souls in his sword are released and go toward that door, they ask Emmanual to open it completely.

Emmanual opens that door and another spirit comes out and says "thanks for releasing me, I was trapped in there for the last 10,000 years, I don't have much time here now though I have to go to heaven", one of the spirits of Emmanual's sword say "long time no see, Richard". The souls in the sword and Richard keep talking and then Richard sees something and is terrified.

He asks Emmanual "kid where did you get that sword, is that sword perhaps…. The legendary Kanshou No Reikon of the Wailing soul, I was 572 years when I saw that sword I could not even wield it, and you are wielding it at such a young age, how is that possible?! Are you pure enough to wield it? Wait, no way are you Go…." The spirit then vanishes.

As soon as the spirit vanishes Emmanual sees a book covered with dust, he picks it up, removes the dust on top of it. He saw that the book had to tittle it just had a black eye like the one that creature had and a white eye, he never saw a white eye so he was confused and wanted to know more about it.

He opens the book to read it and then he sees a picture of that creature on the first page itself, he reads more about it only to find out that the creature he saw was the devil and he controlled everything in the demon realm and he had black eyes.

He reads more about the devil and his eyes, he finds out that the Black eyes of the devil has different abilities, they were 'the rewrite' it could overwrite the abilities or temporarily stop the ability of the other eyes, 'the echo' it could do the move the enemy is about to do before they do it, and 'the reality rift' which allows the user to travel to different dimensions, realms and even universes.

He also learns that the only the cruellest people can wield that eye he then says "that explains why the devil had that eye, I want it as well, the abilities are really good, if I had that eye I could destroy anyone in battle. I gotta agree though that I got lucky that the person who I fought in the tournament from the yellow school did not use it, I would have lost so easily if he did"

He continues reading about that eye and how to get it, he wanted that eye because it also said that it was a requirement for awakening the legendary sword Kanshou no Reikon, he also learned that his sword was the sword of cruelty wielded by the sun god Amaterasu.

 He continues reading and then he sees that the other half of the book which had information on the white eye was torn and he could not find them. So, he just leaves the book back where it was and goes to meet professor Albert.

Professor Albert asks him "did you find anything about it?" he replies with "no there were no such books". He does not tell professor albert about the information he got about the black eye and the devil.

Ch 14- The swordsmen duo

After reading the book they come back and Emmanual goes back to the red school, he was verry happy to be with Louis again, Louis asks him "nice to see you again bro, school was boring without you, where were you though?"

Emmanual replies "oh, I was researching about my sword, turns out I can awaken it to make myself stronger, I just don't know how to do it." Emmanual does not tell Louis about the black eye.

Louis says "bro I think I am starting to like swords now so I am going to buy a better one so I could keep up with you, and maybe I will get stronger by the next tournament of schools", "let's go, wait, how about we buy matching swords, I think I want to start wielding 2 swords at once, I bet It will look cooler."

They go to the noble district to buy swords, Emmanual who never visited that place is excited to see the different swords. Louis says "okay, so we're here, let's buy two swords that are similar and leave. Don't overdo it this time."

Louis already loses sight of Emmanual and finds him near a sword overwhelmed with his eyes gleaming, Emmanual says "Louis... do you smell that? That's the scent of cured lacquer, polished mahogany, and folded steel. We're standing on sacred ground."

Louis replies with "Here we go again..." Emmanual approaches another sword in a velvet lined case and says "Wait. Look at this one. Look at it, Louis. Do you see the curve? That is no ordinary blade—that's a harmony of weight and intention. The kissaki—the blade's tip—is perfectly aligned with the soul of the metal. The Hamon line isn't just cosmetic... it whispers. You can see the tremble of each fold—it's been through thousands of hammer strikes. This sword isn't made......it's remembered."

Louis stares at Emmanual blankly and says "Uh-huh. Does it cut things?" Emmanual laughs and replies with "Oh, it doesn't just cut. It calls. This blade wants a wielder who doesn't fight out of rage, but out of purpose. Feel the balance—it's as if the sword finishes your movements before you begin them. That right there is a masterpiece"

Louis then says "Okay, cool, cool. But I just want one that matches yours and doesn't break when I smack someone with it." Emmanual points towards a similar blade in the next shelf "This one. Same forge. Same Eather signature. A bit shorter—built for speed and precision. That's your style. We'll be mirror images on the field—like twin storms."

Louis unsheathes it and tests a few swings, he says "Yup. Swings nice. Cuts air. Doesn't feel cursed. I'll take it." Emmanual sighs and says "One day you'll see the poetry in steel, my friend." Louis replies with "And one day you'll stop flirting with swords.", Emmanual laughs and says "ha, never happening, not in a million years"

Louis wanted to buy 2 swords and wield both of them at once just like Emmanual, he searches for a while in the shop but finds nothing good.

Louis sighs and says "Alright, I give up. Emmanual, just pick one for me. You're the sword nerd here. I'll probably end up grabbing something cursed if I choose it myself."

Emmanual turns around slowly in disbelief and says "no way. You're... giving me full authority?" louis replies with "Yes. Full authority. Just don't give me something that's too heavy, too weird, or possessed." Emmanual in a serious tone says "Understood."

He walks over to a stand near the centre of the shop. His fingers hover just above a katana, then a wakizashi, then something longer—he's scanning, breathing with each blade.

He continues searching for a while and then he stops at a sleek katana encased in deep black lacquer, wrapped in a crimson-and-onyx cord. The blade has a gentle, almost imperceptible curve. The steel glints like frozen moonlight.

Emmanual picks up that sword and says "Louis... this is it. This blade isn't loud. It's quiet confidence. It doesn't scream power—it carries it. See the grain? That's Hada, like wood rings—it shows this sword was folded over a hundred times. It's refined... like you, when you're not talking. The tsuba—the guard—is minimal, meaning no wasted movement. A sword for a thinker. For someone who strikes only when, he's sure. It's fast, light, balanced. Forged for precision. For discipline. This... is your blade."

Louis stares at Emmanual confused and says "You just described a sword better than my mom described me at my birthday party."

Emmanual smiles and says "That's because this sword knows you, Louis. It's not flashy, it's not showy… but in the right hands? It ends fights before they begin." Louis says "okay, that's some cool stuff" Emmanual replies "I know."

Louis picks up the sword and says "It feels right. I don't know what all that 'hada' and 'tsuba' stuff meant… but it feels like mine." Emmanual then says "Perfect. Now we match—my blade is a storm.

Yours is a whisper. Together, we're the entire sky. We shall cut past all or enemies with these", Louis laughs and says "Okay, now let's buy them before you marry yours."

Both of them buy the swords they picked and Emmanual is beyond excited to use these swords in battle.

Louis asks Emmanual "bro what do you find so exciting in swords, they are just pieces of metal beaten into a specific shape" Emmanual replies with, "you won't get it, every sword is a work of art in its own way"

Ch 15- The power behind eyes

After buying those when Louis and Emmanual go to school everyone are startled at how they became such good friends in such a short time.

They go to their class, and professor Erin says "you've got some nice pair of swords" they say "thanks professor"

Professor Erin starts teaching, he says "students, listen up, today we are going to talk about how to increase the percentage of Eather you can use from your eyes, some of you might not know that we only use 3 percent of Eather stored in our eyes"

Emmanual hears that and wonders "no way, only 3 percent, that means I can become way stronger" he carefully listens to what professor Erin says and wants to try using more Eather present in his eyes.

He tries it but does not work, it was so hard that even Louis could only bring it up to 5 percent, Emmanual asks Louis how he did that, then Louis explains it to him, Emmanual tries again and this time he gets it and now can use 4 percent.

Emmanual opens his eyes using 4 percent of the Eather in his eyes. Just him opening his eyes sent a devastating wave of Eather it was strong enough to make a few students in the class unconscious. Emmanual sees that and immediately reverts it back to 3 percent.

Professor Erin says "the most amount of Eather a person has used is 12 percent; the Eather king is the only person who can use 12 percent of the Eather in his eyes.

Emmanual goes to the school ground which was big enough for him to practice using their Eather, since he is a noble, he just rented the entire place.

he starts practicing on Eather dummies which are like normal humans but can regenerate damage from any attack instantly.

While Emmanual was practicing, he realized that he could not increase the amount of Eather he can use to 4 percent, he is stuck at 3 percent. He realizes that there is a strange power stopping him from doing that.

He looks around for a bit and sees a strange figure in an old torn black hood covering his face, Emmanual says "are you the one stopping from using my powers? Just let me practice" the man in the hood starts laughing, Emmanual goes towards him and points his sword onto him and says "stop it, let me practice" that man vanishes and appears on the other side of the ground.

Emmanual goes towards him and he vanishes again. Emmanual regains his powers so he continues practicing.

After practicing for a while he goes back to school and talks about the man in hoodie to professor Erin.

Professor Erin says "oh, that happened to me as well, I reported it to the police, they are investigating, they will find him soon, he is rumoured to be of another nation"

Emmanual then goes to meet Louis, but then he sees that Louis is being bullied by seniors, so Emmanual steps in and picks a fight with the seniors.

Emmanual begins with a thrust but they dodge it so he decides to use an ability of Kanshou no Reikon.

 He starts chanting "Let dread seep through bone and thought. Shadows crawl, and hearts decay. Let terror wear my face. Kanshou no Reikon… Become my wrath!"

He raises his sword up in the air and says "fear incarna…." He stops and sees that Louis opened his eyes and the bullies are thrown away without even Louis trying to attack, he realizes it was Eather released from Louis's eyes that defeated the bullies.

He is shocked and asks "how did you do that?! Are you training secretly without me or something?" Louis says "huh? I did that? I don't remember anything like that" Emmanual explains Louis what happened Louis is shocked. He does not believe that he defeated them.

Emmanual and louis hang out for some time and Emmanual tells Louis about the man in the hood that stopped him from using his powers to the fullest.

They go back to their home and see a gold coated letter from the king, they opened it and it said that there was a court guard special practice for future wars, it was a ceremony held by the king to test the strength of the court guards.

In that ceremony the court guards had to divide in teams of 2 and fight the strongest people of the country. Emmanual and louis wanted to be on the same team, because they wanted to test the powers of their new swords.

They headed towards the palace for the court guard ceremony, the host explains them the rules and the different levels of the ceremony, the more they win, their opponents get more stronger and there are 10 levels they have to clear in this ceremony.

The ceremony starts but this time it was a private ceremony so there were only a few spectators, this was very beneficial since that did not make Louis and Emmanual nervous and they were really confident this time because the king himself was watching every match.

The ceremony starts and Louis and Emmanual easily clear the first 4 levels and it is the 5th floor that causes them trouble. Their opponent was also a swordsman and had the green eye and the red eye.

Every move of theirs was being predicted and they could not even do anything. They tried everything they can, they even combined their Eather together to create a combined attack released from their swords at the same time, but that did not do much damage to him, their opponent was not defeated yet, he just was not able to move for some time.

Emmanual raises his sword and chants "In the silence between breaths, I call the blade of judgment. Not of flesh— but of soul and sin. Kanshou no Reikon... Cut where life dares not."

Emmanual points his sword towards his enemy and says "ROAR, **soul sever**", their opponent's soul is completely annihilated and he just falls to the ground. He had to be carried out by the doctors.

Emmanual says "that's 5 levels cleared, the other 5 are going to be harder, we only have time till tomorrow to practice, the other 5 are going to be tomorrow, we have to do this Louis"

Emmanual continues talking and wanted to ask Louis why his eyes turned black for a second in the battle, but he thinks he just hallucinated or something and brushes it off.

The next day when they go for the ceremony, they had to clear 5 more levels. They started continuing the ceremony on the 6th level.

It was not looking good for Emmanual and Louis since their opponent was stronger than anyone they have fought, nothing was working against him and he was dodging everything.

That is when Louis shouts and looks at Emmanual with a demonic look and his eyes were black.

Louis starts attacking Emmanual and Emmanual realizes that he is not able to use 4 percent of his Eather and he is stuck at 3 percent. Louis shouts and says "I won't let you get full control, get out of my body"

Emmanual realizes that something is wrong, so he tries to read Louis's mind but he could not do that since there was absolute darkness in one half and normal in the other half.

The higher-ups realize that there was a spirit of someone inside Louis, they rush to the ground, and the spirit in Louis says "Emmanual, guess who your real dad is, I bet you can't" Emmanual replies "shut up I know who my dad is, I bet you don't even know who your dad is"

The higher ups are flung away by the Eather released so Emmanual has to do something, he starts chanting "Bound in flesh, bound in fear—I unchain the flame behind your eyes. Screaming soul, return to the void, Or dwell forever in *Kanshou no Reikon.*"

 A few spirits appear and hold Louis's physical and spiritual body and Louis is rendered immobile for a while, then the spirit extractors come and remove the spirit inside Louis.

The spirit extracted from Louis's body was too strong to be destroyed, they tried questioning it, asking its name and where it came from but the spirit refused to answer. And ran away into the sky.

Emmanual confronts Louis and asks him "why did that spirit go into you?" Louis replies "I don't know, it was trying to tell me something about you, but I couldn't understand what he was saying"

Louis then suddenly falls on the ground, completely unconscious, Emmanual picks him up and takes him to the hospital.

The ceremony they had looked forward to was postponed and moved to a later date. Both Emmanual and Louis were disappointed when they heard this news since they spent many hours and a lot of hard work completing five tough stages.

They invested everything they had into practicing, trained their butts off, and it was demoralizing to think about waiting who knows how long before they could represent what they did.

However, rather than allowing the letdown to take hold of them, Emmanual and Louis agreed to stay on course. This could potentially be a blessing in disguise, after all, who knows the whole future? They quickly made a plan to ramp up their training. The commitment to training now was clear. They would get more time to refine skills, plan strategies, and develop team chemistry.

They met Monday through Wednesday nightly and practiced in evening trials. They practiced playing upside down, on low batter time, with all sorts of challenge rules. They pored over each other's strengths and appreciated all they brought to the team.

The time went on, and as they continued to show up for their practices, they started to feel more alike good buddies and good partners. They started

looking at this whole ordeal as a good opportunity
to up their game.

They were sure that when it was time to do the
ceremony, they would be ready, and would be even
more proud of the work they put in!

Ch 16- A new friend

The next day in school, Emmanual and Louis see a new student, they wonder who that was, they went to their class and professor Erin said "oh yeah, that child, he is a transfer student, and Emmanual, you sit beside him and help him understand everything, you have to help him."

Emmanual sighs and says "fine, I will". He goes towards the new student and says "Yo, I am Emmanual, nice to meet you, what is your name?" the student looks at him and says "nice to meet you, my name is Cifer."

 When Emmanual looks at him, he sees that Cifer has 2 different eye colours, he thinks "he must be strong, gotta test out his strength."

Emmanual tells him everything about the school and as they continue talking, Emmanual thinks that they could be good friends so he introduces him to Louis.

 Cifer also meets Nicholas the three eyed soul in Kanshou no reikon, Nicholas swears to protect Cifer and Louis. Cifer sees the Kanshou no reikon and says "no way you can wield it right, that is a very rare sword" after saying that he stops talking for a while and appears as if he was thinking something deep.

Emmanual asks him "yeah I can wield it, it is not that hard to wield it, do you like swords as well?" he waits for him to respond and says "you there"

 Cifer responds with "yeah I was just thinking about something, and about swords I love them I also wield 2 of them at once like you do"

Emmanual thinks "I definitely did a great job making him my friend" the next thing Louis and Cifer are talking about was cars and anime.

Emmanual says "oh man, I don't know much about cars, but I do about anime" the continue talking and became pretty good friends.

In fact, they talk so good friends that even when professor Erin forbid them from sitting together, they were able to talk.

They decide to go out to eat somewhere, everyone has a different opinion on where to go, so their conversation was not coming to an end, until Louis says "in the noble district there is an anime and car themed café, wanna go there, wait Cifer, are you a noble?"

Cifer says "yeah but I don't know where that is" Louis replies with "oh that is not a problem just come with us."

After school they were on their way to the café and Emmanual and Louis see that Cifer was wearing clothes which were too formal they ask him "bro we are going to a café, why are you wearing something so formal?" he replies "oh this, it is my usual outfit".

Louis and Emmanual are confused since a well-tailored white blazer and matching trousers, paired with a dark-coloured dress shirt underneath is not supposed to be someone's usual outfit.

They just ignore it and continue going towards the café. They were going in a BMW m5 competition which was Louis's favourite car, he was excited to test its top speed, he asks Cifer "can we rev the car please, I love the sound it makes, and where did you buy this? it does not look like the one we get over here"

Cifer replies "oh this, I bought it back when I was in Germany, we can rev it later, there are too many people on the street"

They reach the café and Emmanual finds a worthy opponent who might be able to eat more than him, so they have a competition of who can eat the most, and Emmanual gets the edge.

Louis was truly amazed by how much both of them could eat; they really put it away! As he watched both of his friends gobble there food down, he really couldn't believe how much of an appetite they both had.

They had plates filled to the top with so many different styles of dishes, not to mention the food they ate, while also engaging in conversation and laughter. We truly didn't think they were going to be able to finish their plates.

Then came the bill; everyone was in total shock when they brought the bill over to their table, looking at each other in disbelief from the total.

The prize was unbelievable, and nothing like what they had presumed it would be. But Emmanuel and Louis were dedicated to not paying for it; they started an escape plan to ditch because they should not be accountable for the considerable expense.

Emmanuel with a on his face and Louis, about agreed upon the same time, felt it was time to exit; what was left? when Emmanuel and Louis exited, Cifer was astounded and yelling that they would leave him there and not even pay half of the bill, don't bother running!

By now, there were definitely laughs from everyone, and Louis still chuckling on what just happened as they walked down the sidewalk, satisfied with a very memorable meal experience.

Ch 17-The war begins

The day after swordsmanship class, the excitement and high spirits were palpable when Professor Erin faced her class, and announced another challenge with the goal of improving their combat skills. he stated, firmly but with a light-hearted tone, that they would be sparring with each other in a series of matches. But this wasn't your ordinary practice; it was more like a tournament where they would showcase their skills and encourage each other during matches.

After a few fights Emmanual was doing quite well, made it to the quarter finals, he was up against Cifer.

They had an Eather showdown, both of them released so much Eather that it was enough to badly injure a few students.

They started battling and it was a toe-to-toe battle, until Emmanual unsheathe his kanshou no reikon, the were exchanging a few blows, and Emmanual says "how about you draw out your other sword"

"Nah I am good, I wanna test your strength" says Cifer, everyone was shocked after seeing that both of them have the same fighting style, and think almost the same things at the same time. It was almost like they are twins and are battling.

A deafening blast echoed violently through the air and rattled the ground. No one could understand what they heard; the crowd was frozen for just a moment. They turned in unison to Cifer, who stood in the centre of chaos. He had a certain power about him and looked uneasy; he was back on his feet and surveying the damage. After the dust began settling, they all noticed a distinct scratch across Cifer's face that looked like a red line contrasting against his pale skin. This left Cifer no choice other than unsheathing his other sword.

Now the fight releases even more Eather knocking down everyone except Louis and professor Erin.

Professor Erin asks them to stop fighting since it knocked everyone out and they did not want any more damage. They stop fighting and after a few minutes the people who were knocked out wake up and all of them get confused about what happened to them.

Cifer released more Eather than he should have so he had to go to the doctor to check if his eyes are fine.

That day so much Either was released that the other realms shook, and the demon realm was not so happy about it.

The king of the realm, the Devil himself sought revenge, so he asked the prince of the realm to attack their kingdom.

In the middle of the kingdom, a portal formed. With garish colours and a spinning glow, it beckoned. The prince descended from the demon realm, emerging from the portal in shadowed garb. He arrived with such force that kingdoms felt vibrations in the air, transforming the reign of the day and rendering it clear why he was here. For one brief instance, all halted in wonder and fear.

The court guards raced to the great hall with worry on their faces and the promise of conflict with the influential prince of the demon realm. The environment was unstable, and the air was charged with rage. The guards, as loyal as they come, took up weapons and their fellow guards to defend the demon prince on behalf of their King and their realm. However, just as they were about to defend themselves from the demon prince, the King, a man of great wisdom and bravery, suddenly turned back.

He didn't have to draw his sword. His strength was proof of his power and his skill. He loomed. He appeared as a titan overshadowing an ancient battlefield—the air seemed to vibrate with an unknown emotion.

The earth shook under his feet; the tension in the air was so thick it could have been cut with a knife—all that anyone could do was stand with their mouth agape, frozen by the gravity of his presence.

The shockwaves generated from his presence pervaded the kingdom and beyond, stopping everyone in their tracks.

The fight continued and did destruction, but the King won, he did not even have a scratch after the battle. He made scars on the body of the prince which will last forever.

Nonetheless, despite the King winning the battle, he made the right choice not to slay the prince. As an enemy, he was a member of the noble family of the realm next to theirs, killing him would likely have led to a war of destruction.

Even in a time of war, killing the leaders of other realms could have disastrous repercussions by throwing their kingdoms into war which would affect countless innocents. The King was aware of the tenuous balance of power that existed between the kingdoms, and recognized that a single lapse in judgment could undo work on international relations that was sometimes decades in the making.

After the war, when Emmanual and Louis went to visit Cifer in the hospital they saw that he had a few scars on his body because the hospital was near the place the battle happened, and the staff in the hospital also had huge scars just because of the battle.

Cifer was not the only one in the hospital now, there were many other people in the hospital now, most of them were injured just because they were standing close to the place where the battle happened.

After the Devil's utter defeat by the valiant hero, he
was filled with a raging sense of anger and
fury. It was not just an ephemeral feeling.it was
a seething, brooding need for vengeance that ran th
rough his blackened veins.

He had always taken pride in being the
ultimate personification of evil, a power to
be feared, and the ignominy of his defeat ate at him
like a voracious hunger.

Yet, following his defeat,he had discovered himself c
onfronted with an unforeseen and confounding dile
mma: for reasons beyond his comprehension, he
had lost half of his powers temporarily.

Ch 18- The Grand Historian

It had been one week since the King had duelled the Demon Prince, an event that had diverted a realm. The sound of clashing blades and wreaking spells had been engraved into people's minds.

An unusual event happened: No wars had emerged from the duel. No armies marched on the horizon and no banners flew in defiance. Therefore, the kingdom existed in a strange, almost eerie peace; the serenity was almost comfortable, yet it felt unsettling.

However, for Emmanual, a once-soldier of the king, such peace was lost as a result of the duel. Each and every night for the last week he found himself tormented by vivid fragments in dreams.

Fragmentary images that felt like Deja vu from a long, lost era hidden at the heart of world, collapsing time and space, yet existing together as shell upon shell of petrified soil.

He wandered through a long, shadowy hallway of obsidian and glass with walls that reflected everything and nothing, filled with disembodied whispers of languages he did not quite know, but were ancient and foreign even if he felt familiarity.

While voices surrounded him, one phrase hung above all lingered in the air while the spirits trapped within Emmanual's sword spoke in fitful reverberation:

"Seek the Archive."

At first, he dismissed it as the by-product of the duel and the stress of the events that had taken place. But on the 7th night, the dreams took on a new level of severity. He woke up sweating violently, his heart racing as if trying to escape his chest. His sword, ordinarily just a weapon of war, was vibrating with an energy he had never felt before—it was almost glowing from the moonlight that was shining through his window. The whispers were louder now, more insistent, as if the universe was urging him.

"You are burdened by three eyes. You have to remember."

The meaning was ambiguous, but he felt it resonate deep down, igniting a spark of determination he had not felt thus far. The next morning, Emmanual made the decision to skip class because there was no resisting the desire to bound into the unknown.

He headed towards the Palace of Eyes, with his devoted companion Louis at his side. When he arrived at the Palace of Eyes he requested a meeting with the Grand Historian, the keeper of all time.

An old woman greeted them with an air of wisdom that seemed to transcend time itself.

She walked with a cane carved from driftwood, each step resonating like a heartbeat against the stone floor. Her eyes—one red, one yellow—were calm yet sharp, piercing through the veil of uncertainty that surrounded Emmanual.
"Three-eyed child," she said without surprise, as if she had been expecting him. "You've come for the Archive."
"You... know?" Emmanual stammered, caught off guard by her awareness.
"I know more than your professors ever will," she replied cryptically. "Come with me."

With that, she took them down into the earth, into a series of tunnels that had not been walked for millennia. The tunnels were carved with strange shapes and symbols that changed as they walked—first they were polished stone, but quickly deteriorated to some ancient strange form—as if they were walking into the depth of the earth. The air became cooler, thick with the essence of time.

Eventually, they came upon a large room without doors or windows; only a mirror stabilized in the midst of the room. The mirror was pristine; untarnished by dust or time.

"This is the entrance." She said softly to them, her voice echoing in the stillness. "But your eyes must open it."

Emmanual had walked towards the mirror and could feel the electricity in the air. When he stepped closer, the red, blue, and green eyes flickered to life, glowing as if he had activated a light that had been dormant for a long time.

Suddenly, the mirror began to melt in front of him, the surface warping like water, exposing a passage through the mirror.

This was it, they could not turn back now - they were diving into the depths of the unknown, a world that held secrets waiting to be unearthed.

Emmanual took a breath, looked at Louis, and walked forward to find out what was beyond.

Inside, time had no meaning. Books floated in the air, defying gravity, as they levitated in space with no visible means of support.

Lights flickered and pulsed randomly without any apparent mechanism, creating a hazy dimness with elongated shadows, weaving across the walls.

Everything was weightless, enveloped in deep silence, and magical tranquillity that felt strange and unsettling.

There, in the very centre of the room, was a huge, luminous sphere made from crystal. It must have been four, maybe five, times bigger than a human; it towered over its surroundings like a house. Inside, caught in a crystalline cage—frozen—was a man suspended in the singularity of time. He had three eyes like Emmanual.

Louis stepped back, his heart pounding. "Is that...?"

The Grand Historian solemnly nodded. "That is Eon. The first Eye King. Just like Emmanual and Nicholas, a swordsman from the past."

Emmanual's sword throbbed with that strange energy again.

"He's not dead," she explained, sounding calm. "He's sealed. Not because he was evil... but because he knew something we weren't ready to learn."

Emmanual sensed an unexplainable pull toward the crystal. When he touched the cool surface with his hand, images began to flood into his mind—images of other worlds, other timelines, and a strange white eye looking back at him.

He jolted awake in a panic, heart racing as if he'd just completed a marathon. Doppelganger shadows lingered in the corners feeling as if they were alive, almost like the eerie sensation of something just unbeknownst beyond his field of vision.

"It's coming," he said, body trembling uncontrollably, still grasping for the remnants of the nightmare that possessed him. The images still felt vivid and felt awful, the awful confusion and panic swirling into a dark vortex of dread. They felt far too real to just shake off.

Louis looked at him, his eyes moving quickly across his friend's face, brows furrowed in concern - the expression of dread graven into his friend's face and eyes. "What do you mean?" he asked along a line of curiosity and caution. The air in the room felt charged - the weight of unsaid fears and unidentified anxieties, coursing in waves through the atmosphere like pulsating door bells, or a rippling blanket of charged energy.

 Louis realized, I need to help, how do I even cope with that, how do I comfort a being in a deeper psycho-emotional state than I had never encountered?

As they walked through the familiar doors of the library, a sense of anticipation hung in the air. Sunshine flooded through the tall windows, spreading a golden hue across the polished wooden floors sat the tranquillity of the past felt almost alive.

As if they were not there out of curiosity, but out of some omnipresent force that was compelling them to know what truth had transpired in their dream.

The continued echoes of their own whispers almost seemed to join the soft rustling of pages from other corners of the room, using those echoes they begin their search for the reference section where the grand historian was said to be standing.

As they walked the dream weighed on their mind heavily, still vivid in their mind it felt impossible to distinguish reality from imagination. Trade-off knowing glances of excitement and apprehension that gave them shivers from having such a memory.

As they stumbled in the direction they thought the area would be, there stood the grand historian, just as much enchanting as he was in their dream; with his long and regal robe, hair and beard flowing, that seemed to billow slightly in air stillness.

They were shocked that the same thing that happened in the dream was happening right in front of them, they are escorted toward the mirror, and it melts just like the dream and they enter.

Emmanual's kanshou no Reikon starts glowing and he sees his reflection in which he has an extra eye hole, where there was space for another eye.

When he asks Louis if there is an eye hole above his forehead, Louis vehemently says no, shaking his head with uncertainty and fear. Emmanuel is now even more baffled and confused. It's like he felt there is clearly something more to this than he was actually able to see, literally.

Not able to stop the flood of insatiable exploration, Emmanuel closes his eyes and immediately finds himself lost in the bounds of his mind. Without warning, he is seeing literal memories belonging to the first Eye King, Eon.

Views upon views play in memory-like fashion, revealing not only the story of Eon, but the struggles he endured. Emmanuel sees Cedric situated, in the distance rests an ancient, wondrous landscape before him, the weight of the crown clearly weighing down on his shoulders.

He secures more and more memories as, step-by-step, they appear for him to digest, and illustrate Eon's struggle for power, sacrifice, and important wisdom he gained while suffering among a world full of treason and betrayal.

As Emmanuel takes in these memories, he begins to understand the significance of the eye holes, their relation to Eon's legacy, and what could happen because they are there. The truth of the Eye King and his powers starts to reveal itself and leaves Emmanuel with more questions than he is getting answered.

He sees the memories of the Eye king Cedric and tells about them to the grand historian, she said "no way, this can't be possible, you are the reincarnation of the first Eye King Eon, I can't tell you anything more about him, there is no information about him, no one knows anything about him and his story"

Emmanual sincerely does not believe it; despite all the evidence he has been shown. He has a longing inside that he has waited a long time for, a hope that he will be something great, and of course, the ambition he has for himself of being the Eye King keeps burning inside him.

 In his sight of his life's journey, he sees a future where he leads a great kingdom of people, who respect him and look up to him, for the power of his mind and body.

Every day, he trains hard, pushes things under control and prepares for every step he could take on his journey. He needs to become the Eye King, he knows this. Will this be an easy journey? No, but with each obstacle, he only grows stronger.

Emmanual sees visions of being the holder of the Eye of Power, a great object that gives view and insight to its holder. Emmanual's ambition is not just for his fame, he just wishes to push the people up and bring them all together when they are together to live a new life. He feels he was meant for this, and nothing will stop him from making his dreams come true.

They walk back in the direction of the hospital where Cifer was taken for treatment, the weight of apprehension and uncertainty pressing down on them.

With the smell of antiseptic all around them, they navigate their way through the stark white hallways, every step weighing heavier as their unease builds. Finally, they arrive at his room and find Cifer upright in bed, his face drawn but resolute, a hint of hope in his eyes.

"Cifer," one of them starts, letting out a breath to clear their head. "We need to talk to you." Cifer looks up, a sign of intrigue on his face. They surround him, a collection of concern and urgency.

The news they share is unbelievable; they have met the grand historian, the epic one steeped in gospel, and now they have been told something shocking. Emmanual, a name that has always had an air of inevitability, is not just a random person.

The grand historian told them that Emmanual is a reincarnated version of the first Eye King, a powerful monarch from some unknown antiquity, who had wisdom and knowledge beyond comprehension.

At first, Cifer does not believe it. He shakes his head slowly as if the weight of the journey is heavy. "You are not serious," he whispers weakly. "How is that even possible?" The only sound in the hospital room is the soft hum of the machines on Cifers body.

They all look, the friends understand what they are saying and have a moment of clarity, they remember the words of the grand historian, how he spoke the words so simply and as if he was passing a reasonable fact. "The way he expressed certainty. His eyes. The sudden wealth of knowledge exploded onto us as if he were a human avalanche."

They tell him that in his past the stories of Emmanual life were everlasting tales of courage, leadership, and an absolute commitment to justice.

Cifer listens carefully, battling within himself between doubt and the glimmer of hope that is beginning to form. "But what does this mean for us? For him?" he asks, attempting to make sense of the complex emotions swirling around in his mind. The revelation has massive implications and everyone knows this is just the starting point of a journey that could change everything in their lives.

They turned to Professor Erin with excitement and curiosity about the mysterious history of the Eye Kings. When they crowded around her desk, it was all they could do to contain their excitement. At that moment in time, there was no more authoritative figure on the place of the Eye Kings than Professor Erin.

She had a razor-sharp mind on a multitude of subjects and had also done some substantial research on the topic, and she was considered a beacon of understanding in a field that had left others baffled.

However, when they asked about the first Eye King Eon, the room fell silent. Professor Erin worked her brow and let a few seconds pass looking for something in her mind she could reflect back on.

Eventually, the darkness of silence transitioned into light when she said, "I'm not sure I know much about the first Eye King." She seemed to struggle with the fact that she had to utter the phrase "I'm not sure" aloud.

The students looked at each other and quickly transitioned from shock and disappointment from revealing that Professor Erin had no information to share about such an important figure. How can a scholar of her Caliber be clueless about such an important event?

They were shocked, even Moreso, because she had always been their beacon of light revealing hidden knowledge and bringing clarity to important issues, and there she was devoid of any information.

Surprisingly, the lack of knowledge of the first Eye King Eon felt like a bigger mystery than anyone could have imagined. This discovery led them to a new resolve; they would start their own search for answers.

Maybe there was some truth that an answer had never been provided or uncovered; maybe the most brilliant of minds had missed it too.

A boldness of sorts surged inside them to search for answers to the first Eye King Eon. The discovery of a "bigger" question ignited a curiosity fuel that no one could extinguish, and it would propel them into the unknown, and the search for the first Eye King.

Ch 19- The treasure in the library

The following day, Emmanual and Louis took a day trip to the library, as they had an unquenchable curiosity and were compelled to find out more about the first Eye King, Eon.

They walked through the same area where the mystical mirror resided, the very portal in which they travelled via some fantastical adventure just a day before.

Eagerly, yet pensively, they stepped through the mirror-like surface once again and clogged their noses with more of the cold and adrenaline enough to feel almost nauseous.

When they came out of the other side, they were in a deep cave that had the echoes of ancient spirits. It was dark, with glowing smudges lighting the dark canvass, and they felt heavy and soothed, a presence of time and history pulsated through the air.

 The further they went into the cave, the more they felt the true presence of Eon, the depths of their imaginings, and the swirling energies they were absorbing from him.

The walls of the cave were covered in detailed carvings and pictures of the life and times of Eon's first Eye King. Emmanual and Louis were caught up in the artistry, their minds swirling with questions of Eon's time, his powers and the difficulties he faced in an attempt to protect the realms.

Each carving seemed to tell a story, and as they closely examined the artwork, the more captivated they became with the actual history.

They went even deeper into the cave, and it was completely lit up by an unknown source of light. The Kanshou no Reikon started glowing even brighter.

They continued deeper into the past, into the old cave, with their torches flickering against the wet stone, casting strange shadows that seemed to swirl around them.

Then they found a beautiful sword stuck in the ground where they were. The sword was the most beautiful sword any of them had ever seen.

The sword had beautiful designs, and from them it radiated a power that felt different. The sword sparkled with a disconcerting yet captivating lustre that spoke of the struggles and events it had seen over the years. The air about it felt alive, as if the sword had a life of its own, and it was waiting for the right hands to unleash its formidable power.

They ask the grand historian about the sword and she says "that is the legendary sword, moon blossom, the blade that has never killed, it could cut through curses, dispel hatred, and even heal spiritual wounds. It was said the sword would never draw blood unless the wielder's heart was pure and merciful."

While the grand historian was talking, Emmanual went up to the sword and unsheathed it, and says "looks like a good sword" right after he said that, the grand historian says "you were not supposed to unsheathe it you DUMBASS!!"

Emmanual confused asks her why and she says "all of its wielders had a random curse forever", Emmanual relieved says "oh curse, I don't believe in such shit, even if it does we will see about that later, and why did you swear at me?" the historian says "I don't give a fuck, just put the sword back and, GET OUT!!!!"

Emmanuel, attracted by the shimmering blade of the sword, suddenly found himself lost in admiration. The intricate carving sparkled under the light, drawing his attention completely away from the Grand Historian, who was deeply engrossed in recounting the tales of ancient artifacts.

 Seizing the opportunity, Emmanuel skilfully executed a clever switch. With a fast and discreet motion, he carefully removed the moon blossom from its cover and replaced it with Louis's sword, which had been resting nearby.

The Grand Historian, oblivious to the change, continued his narration, unaware that the precious moon blossom was now hidden away.

Meanwhile, Emmanuel, feeling a rush of adrenaline, stepped back to admire his handiwork and the gleaming sword that now occupied the moon blossom's former place.

Emmanual and Louis snuck out of the library with the moon blossom they had fought hard to obtain, and Louis was furious. He was furious, and in his angry exclamation that he had lost his favourite sword, he was already red in the face.

Louis began shouting at Emmanual, and Emmanual simply responded calmly, and coolly, once again assuring him that it was already taken care of. In fact, Emmanual reported, he had just purchased Louis a new sword, and it was even better than the last one.

Louis's eyes showed just a flicker of surprise, and his sense of fury had at least momentarily subsided to consider the unexpected gift.

Ch 20- A Huge Loss

Emmanual and Louis raced to the hospital, nerves buzzing with excitement and concern about their friend Cifer, who was recovering from an unfortunate illness.

 As they entered the cold and quiet room, they felt relief and concern when seeing Cifer in the hospital bed. After a few greetings, Emmanual and Louis paused.

They knew they had important information to disclose. Emmanual and Louis leaned in closer and lowered their voices while telling Cifer they had taken the legendary Moon Blossom sword, which was stashed in the library, without telling anyone.

They weren't ignorant of what they had done and knew it had consequences. Cifer's eyes widened with shock and perturbation. He was always fascinated by the Moon Blossom sword and its legacy, with much mythology about its power and purpose. Here they were, with two conflicting realities: the excitement of the Moon Blossom sword versus the moral implications of it all.

The weight of what they had done was hitting them hard, and now all they could do was wait for Cifer's response, which could change their lives entirely.

Cifer said "that is the sword that has never killed, better treasure it". Emmanual was still wondering what the curse could be.

They talked to Cifer about school for a bit and left the hospital. They noticed that Cifer was acting weird today and that it just did not feel right.

On that day, Cifer got away from the hospital under the cover of darkness as he slipped out without anyone noticing because the medical staff was so busy with procedures.

As he walked through the semi-darkness of the hallways, he could feel adrenaline and fear coursing through his veins. In those sterile walls, everyone was wondering where he had gone. The doctors and nurses, typically caring for their patients, were baffled by Cifer's departure.

Cifer had been critical. He had experienced substantial injuries desperately in need of constant monitoring and care. His departure created shockwaves of concern throughout the hospital as they became instantly aware they weren't only worried about a simple case of a missing patient, but a person in need of urgent medical care. As they realized their loss, each minute of worry increased as they began to question what had just occurred.

Emmanual and Louis did not know about Cifer's disappearance yet, and were just studying in their houses. A few hours later when they decided to hang out they decided to meet up near a coffee shop in the noble district.

As Louis travelled, he came across an open cave that seemed abandoned because he didn't see any workers, but he did observe someone sitting nearby, lost in thought, quite close to a glowing pool of molten lava. Louis was curious and moved closer, his heart beating slightly faster in his chest.

 As he got closer, he recognized it was Cifer,. Cifer surprised Louis because he had an alarming, demonic appearance about him that sent a chill through Louis's body.

 The stone formations and glowing lava cast flickering light upon Cifer, and in the light, the shadows created by the flickering lava exaggerated the cheekbones and emphasized Cifer's eyes.

Louis was both curious and fearful, especially when he thought about where Cifer ended up and what dreadful thoughts may have been trickling through Cifer's mind.

Cifer looked intensely up at Louis and, in a mumble, began to say something under his breath. The combined sounds that fell from his lips were flowing in some kind of rhythmic manner. He seemed to be speaking to some kind of a deep magic or forgotten spell. Louis was confused and intrigued and tried to stop Cifer to ask "where he was going with this," or something similar.

He had hoped to understand the significance of this moment. But it was clear Cifer was in another universe or dimension somewhere and he was not in the right frequency to interact with. Cifer went on saying phrases and rhythms of words that Louis did not and probably would never understand.

Cifer immersed in the tones, Louis meekly waited, hoping for a response. As he waited stunned and somewhat transfixed, much like a child watching a magician, he began to feel somewhat concerned about the effects of what was proceeding before him. At this point, it became very apparent that Cifer did not have any indication of ever being done with his unique utterances.

Louis asked Cifer many times if he wanted to come with them to the café for a leisurely afternoon, but Cifer remained concentrated and absorbed in his thoughts.

He was chanting continuously, lost in a world of his own. Louis could see that Cifer was in a state of intense focus, almost as if he were tapping into some hidden energy source. Despite Louis's repeated invitations and the enticing aroma of coffee and pastries wafting through the air, Cifer seemed oblivious to it all, committed to his practice and unwilling to break his concentration.

After some time Cifer stopped for a while, stood up and was about to jump into the pool of lava, Louis was still confused and was not understanding what Cifer was doing.

After Louis realized Cifer had almost jumped into the pool of lava, Louis held Cifer's hand to pull him back but Cifer said that it was a part of the ritual and cut his hand and burned in the pool of lava.

This event took place with zero witnesses and with only silence—eerily, that leaves no confirmation. By the time Louis shakily and almost incoherently called Emmanual and the police to report Cifer's death, they didn't know who he was or care what he said. They dismissed him and the truth he tried to convey about an unforeseeable tragedy as unreasonable.

Instead of being cared for as a friend grieving loss, they acted towards him with scepticism, and as though he were a suspect. From there, the situation intensified so dramatically and so swiftly that Louis could hardly tell you what took place.

All he could feel was immense indignation at the injustice - now thinking of being handcuffed and taken to jail. Although completely confused and feeling as if life had turned inside out in a matter of moments, Louis was not able to understand anything and was completely moved by that situation, A horrible situation that involved not only losing a friend but now proving that he did not murder him.

Emmanual asks Louis "why? Just why did you kill Cifer? Were you jealous? Huh? Tell me!!!" Louis was still not able to believe that Cifer died right in front of him, he did not even answer Emmanual.

Cifer's tragic death irrevocably broke the bond between Emmanual and Louis. They were both submerged in a sadness that left them immobilized and struggling to comprehend what had occurred. Emmanual was particularly distressed, finding it hard to process that Cifer had actually died when he remembered all of the times they had shared together.

 He was shocked and trying to understand how someone so full of life could decide to end his life. He had to let go of the questions that plagued him because logically there was no explanation for what had happened.

The weight of the loss was heavy, especially on Emmanual's heart and he couldn't even consider reaching out to Louis as he too was experiencing the weight of the tragedy. The loss felt like an empty void in between the both of them filled with things they would never say to each other.

As the investigations proceeded, the police discovered an alarming number of unanswered questions. Despite their exhaustive investigation, they had not turned up any relevant evidence or leads in relation to the death of Cifer.

The ambivalence of the circumstances surrounding it remained unclear, to the chagrin of all those working the case. In addition, the police were trying to make sense of how Louis had gotten caught up in the terrible situation, whether there was a motive they had been unable to pin down, or if Louis was simply an innocent bystander who had been scapegoated in a greater complexity of the situation.

Each day the case was muddied, and the detectives were determined to dive deeper and get to the bottom. The community was eager for answers, the pressure mounted without any grounding or direction in the investigation.

Time was against the police and the need for resolution compelled common ground for a mystery that left many, including the police tangled and perplexed.

Louis remained in custody for several months and started to feel that the situation could not get any worse. The police searched and searched for evidence of Louis' involvement in the death of Cifer and they found nothing.

The fact that they could not show any direct evidence exacerbated the already anxiety-loaded situation in Louis' case. Meanwhile, Louis found himself socially isolated, cut off from the outside world. He could not communicate with his family, nor could his family visit him during this hard time for them. This naturally took a toll on Louis' mental health and he felt lonely and unwanted.

 The absence of loved ones made his time in jail seem longer and scarier as he faced the fear of being wrongfully accused along with the public scrutiny he faced.

Ch 21- The Sad News

Emmanuel was still entirely unable to cope with the loss of Cifer, his friend. The loss was a heavy weight on his heart and his mind was continually plagued with the memories they had shared. Cifer had been more than a friend; he had been a confidante and a date.

The instantaneously of Cifer's death was still incomprehensible to Emmanuel. He was in denial, missing his best friend, and now he had to deal with the realization of death.

Even worse and confusing and painful for Emmanuel was the fact that Louis, a person he had known for years, was responsible for Cifer's death. Emmanuel just couldn't believe it; it felt like a sick joke.

Louis was part of their group, a guy who friends with them and shared laughs and experiences with Cifer and Emmanuel. It was unbelievable to Emmanuel, that Louis could do this. He couldn't shake the small hope in his heart that told him things may be better than they appeared.

Emmanuel assumed there had to be a reasonable explanation for Louis's behaviour, some rationale that could shed light on the unexpected.

 Maybe Louis was forced, or there were events or experiences combined with immense temptation that led him to such horrific circumstances.

 Each time he thought of the situation, Emmanuel felt overwhelmed with powerful surrounding emotions... anger, sorrow, bewilderment and an all-encompassing wish for clarity.

He simply couldn't bring himself to believe Louis has become the world's villain, so until he found the truth behind the tragedy, he would keep finding comfort in the fact that he had lost Cifer. The loss of Cifer and the betrayal of Louis will follow Emmanuel for a long time.

Despite the unfortunate death of one of his friends, he had learned a very big lesson: Life does not stop because of someone's death. He felt very devastated, but realized that The Earth was still on its axis and people still lived their lives.

This very painful lesson left him feeling somewhat isolated; his heart was broken, and his mind was filled with memories while everyone else's day to day lives went on as usual.

It was a distinct realization of how much bigger grief can seem though it still falls within the confines of a larger society that keeps going.

He looked for support from his dad with hope and a desperate request for wisdom after his loss. When he described his circumstances to his dad and why he reached out, his father said, "So you learned it the hard way, huh? Listen, son, life is not fair." Those were the wise words he needed.

In a simple statement, he had a truth that everyone knows: sometimes life makes us play with cards we do not want. It was a lesson he had to go to school for; it was a school that many people in their own experiences have whatever way they had the same thing happen at some time or another.

He was completely bored; it felt like time had stood still. There was no one to talk to, and the silence around him was overwhelming. Cifer was dead, a lost that left obvious vacuums in his life. Louis was in prison, Jamie thought he was serving a sentence that was somewhat unfair.

The absence of those two weighed heavily on his heart; it made social interaction feel impossible in such a way that the prospect was unbearable. The life outside felt stark and lonely; he wished for any escape from the grimness of the reality around him.

Seeking comfort, he chose to go to the library, a place that had always provided him an outlet in hard times. Just thinking of being with books brought a sense of comfort; his library was a world where he could catch up on the struggles, victories, and failures of characters who faced problems much more serious than his own.

He entered the library; the familiar smell of old paper and leather binding welcomed him like an old friend. He still hoped he could find some distance from his worries and perhaps to even mitigate the stress that was planted firmly in his mind.

He was in his home, a place he could lose himself in stories and maybe find a thrill of inspiration out of the rubble of despair he found himself in.

He was just sitting on the couch, feeling completely empty and blank, as overwhelming sadness washed over him. It seemed everything was spinning around him, while he was stuck in a moment of despair, unable to comprehend what had just happened.

It felt as if his thoughts were tightly balled up like leaves blowing in a windstorm. Seconds felt like hours, and without understanding of the chaos he felt consumed by the confusion, sadness, and numbness.

In an attempt to rid himself of the weight pressing on him, he looked around the room. His eyes landed on the many bookshelves that lined the walls. They were full of books spanning every genre. Each one of them contained a story waiting to be read; he didn't care to read any of them though.

At last, he settled on the books labelled Unsolved Mysteries. There was something about the unknown, and it provided a kind of excitement of adventure that may help crawl him out of the depths of all the mystery and uncertainty existing in his own life.

He opens the book, its old pages brittle and worn. On the first page itself, he sees a bright illustration of a pool of lava, strangely similar to the one in which Cifer died. The fiery colours swirl out at him, captivating him in its beauty and treacherous nature. As he studies the page, the illustration has text that he reads.

The text describes a ritual, an ancient ritual that may be performed to gain enormous amounts of power and strength. The words appear to swirl and dance as he looks at the page explaining not only the process to perform this mystifying ancient ritual, but the benefits and hazards.

He's torn between excitement and apprehension as he considers the knowledge he's just absorbed. The possibility of having so much power revitalizes his ambition and gives him an itch to see if he is durable enough to take on this proposal.

But he does not let that ambition take over and, he did not want to choose the bad path just to gain strength. Suddenly, the book feels heavier; as if it holds more than knowledge; maybe even fate. As he keeps reading the page-turner book, an impatience builds within him. Every page he flips adds another layer to story, pulling him deeper into the thrilling maelstrom of characters' motivations.

He quickly realizes Louis, who at a glance looked like a bad guy, was actually innocent. The bad guy was Cifer, and his dark ambitions caused him to bundle off on some awful ritual to amplify his own capabilities and power. Obviously, it is more than an awful ritual; it demands horrible offerings and horrible elements, finally leading Cifer to mindlessly throw himself into a pool of lava.

Emmanual shifts through horror and fascination as he unravels the truth of Cifer's progression. The lava, which swallows you whole into a burning abyss, reveals the perilous paths Cifer was willing to take to gain strength.

As the story evolves, he contemplates the morality behind the characters' choices. Louis, in spite of being wrongfully accused is still a tragic figure in the scheme of Cifer's warped ambition.

 The protagonist's heart beats faster as he considers the ramifications of this development, compelled to share these understanding with those who may wrongly judge Louis.

It is more than just a story of good and evil; it is a look into innocence, sacrifice, and the true cost of power.

He hires a lawyer and tells him about it; they go the police and prove it to them that Louis was innocent and that Cifer was doing a ritual just to get stronger.

They were finally able to free Louis and they were still wondering why Cifer did that ritual and died on his own will. The investigation continued and they were still searching for Cifer.

Ch 22- The Stuck Dragon

Now that Louis was exonerated from culpability of Cifer's doom, Emmanual was happy to have a study companion, who was most enthusiastic about studying the mystery of what was going on with Cifer.

The two again had the opportunity of company on the journey to the library, as they were used to meeting there independently to consider the reasons why anyone would do something so strange as Cifer had done with the bizarre ritual and claim to leap into the pool of lava.

The expedition through the impressive stacks of the library was accompanied by both excitement and trepidation. The tactile methodologies of knowing are so much more proximate in a library with its scent of monitored decay and the rustling, shuffling sound of pages turning.

Louis and Emmanual's destination was a shelf of books piled in corners, with a ratio of books variously commemorated regarding ancient events and local legends.

Emmanual could not help but think that if they could determine the reasons for Cifer's resolution, they may not only end the mystery of the awful incident but gain insight into some of the more sinister dimensions of their own company.

Each book elicited lost, secret knowledge from sub-conscious recordings, uneasy interests, and a growing need to connect action and consequence in terms of motivations people claim when making such a dramatic choice. They wanted to tell a story that seemed to suspend reason and compelled urgency and curiosity.

They had researched extensively about the ritual that Cifer carried out, searching for anything potentially fruitful, or of interest, to find out what it meant, and, unfortunately for them, they found nothing that would help answer their questions.

They had been in the dimmed library, full of dusty tomes and scrolls, for the last four hours, searching the numerous piles of texts and manuscripts.

They searched through themes old and new, from arcane rituals no one in their right mind would attempt, to moments from history where similar rituals occurred, but nothing on the meaning they had hoped for.

While consuming hours in the haze of scrolling research, when it was clear they would not reach their goal for the day, they decided (with great frustration) it was time to leave.

Tired and tired, they left the library, each of them wondering if they would ever find the answers about Cifer, and what he did.

The next day they go to the library again and start searching about the ritual again, and this time they had a different approach, this time they decided that Louis would go into the cave in which the found the moon blossom, and Emmanual will search in the library.

They tell that to the grand historian and she says "again! This is the third fucking time" Emmanual says "please, we wanna search for something"

They try convincing her and after sometime she agrees after a lot of tries. Louis goes into the mysterious cave and starts searching to see if he finds anything.

He goes to the place where fake moon blossom which the grand historian thinks is the real moon blossom, and he finds a book giving information about the moon blossom and says "oh this will be helpful for Emmanual, I will take it"

The further he goes into the cave, the darkness from the opening fades, and total darkness envelops him so he can see nothing but blackness.

 He feels the cool dampness in the air on his skin, the soft echo of moisture, like a drip, somewhere far in the caverns. At a moment of resolve, he digs into his backpack and pulls out a reliable torch, and relief hits him. "I knew this would come in handy", he thinks to himself, recalling the various adventures he'd taken before.

He clicks the switch and, like a knife through black, the light is penetrating. Not only does he see that the rough stone walls of the cave go up 20 feet and over 30 feet wide, but deep in the blackness, there is something massive.

 As he examines, he realizes this massive figure has an unblinking eye. He jolted backward in fright, feeling terrified as if the nothing in front of him was thinking and watching him.

He gets terrified and turns it off immediately, an unusually fast wind blows, it was like a huge creature was breathing heavily. He hears a very deep voice saying "which motherfucker pointed that torch toward me"

Louis terrified summons Nicholas the three-eyed soul for help, Nicholas appears out of thin air and sees that huge creature and starts attacking

Nicholas continues his fierce onslaught, swinging his sword with total fury, when it suddenly dawns on him that the monstrous creature he is fighting is a dragon. This revelation sends a tremor through him and he takes a deep breath and literally gasps, saying, "I thought dragons went extinct! I had one back in the day, his name was Ignarok!"

 Immediately after he made this declaration, the massive creature abruptly stops its intense attacks, and stares at him with wide, bulging eyes. To Nicholas's amazement, the dragon answered, "Nicholas?! is that you? No way! My name is Ignarok!"

This was such an amazing announcement that Nicholas fell momentarily paralyzed, a torrent of memories from his past adventures with Ignarok flooded his mind, memories which now enveloped him.

Nicholas tells Ignarok, his grand dragon, to stay in the security of the cave. He knows all too well if the dragon steps into the natural world, disaster would occur.

 Seeing such a grand creature flying in the sky, people would either scream in fear or shout in excitement, and many would feel compelled to try to kill it based off fear and ignorance about dragons.

Nicholas sees the value in keeping Ignarok hidden away not just for the sake of the dragon being a dragon, but also to prevent unnecessary confrontations with humans who don't really understand that dragons aren't evil.

This plays a heavy thought for Nicholas, but he knows it's the only way to protect his loyal partner and the naive townspeople nearby.

Louis just watches in disbelief, eyes wide and mind racing as he takes in Nicholas and the enormous dragon that is towering over them. He thought that he had wandered into a dream from where he stood, unable to comprehend what he was seeing. The dragon shimmered, and its scaled skin sparkled like precious, emerald and gold gem stones in the afternoon sun.

 How could it possibly be real? Louis struggled with the actual existence of dragons and other mythological creatures with his logical, critical mind. The air shimmered with electric energy and he could hear the slight rustle of the dragon's wings with it purported changed positions, fixing its piercing glare directly onto him.

 All of the adrenaline in his body screamed for him to run, yet, he remained where he was, frozen in the moment. Nicholas seemed entirely relaxed with the enormous dragon at his side, as if it was a natural thing to have someone interact with a dragon daily. "It's not real", Louis thought, as his heart raced.

As he cautiously moved closer to the amazing creature, he felt a strange combination of excitement and fear. The dragon's scales were iridescent, a beautiful form of deep layers of colours that emphasized its remarkable size.

He brought his hand closer, and as his fingers brushed the cool and smooth texture of the dragon, he felt warmth and energy envelop him. At that moment, he knew it was real, not a figment of his imagination.

He was in awe of the magnificent being before him, and he took pleasure in observing the different complex markings on its skin that displayed strength and majesty.

With a renewed sense of urgency, he turned his attention back to the ancient books and scrolls that were haphazardly laid out around him, wanting to decipher the secrets of the ritual Cifer performed.

He had thousands of questions racing through his mind; was the ritual performed by Cifer to accomplish something, as he immersed himself in research, he felt empowered knowing that if he could understand everything about the ritual, he might be able to understand the dragon and what it represented and could do.

He continued searching about the ritual that Cifer performed and found nothing, so he just asked ignarok the dragon and he knew nothing about that ritual. Nicholas and Louis left and instructed the dragon to stay in the cave.

They chose not to inform the Grand Historian about the dragon and its importance as they were worried it would be too complex, or too risky. They turned instead to Emmanual, hoping he might have come across something of relevance regarding the ancient ritual they were exploring.

 Emmanual shook his head with hint of disappointment. He said he hadn't found anything of particular use. As they walked out of the library, they could feel the weight of their journey pushing down on them.

 It was clear they were frustrated, but there was also a sense of urgency carrying them along. The great shelves with their frivolous knowledge were now laughing at them as they felt their leads were washed away.

Outside the sun was low - it was setting. Long shadows on this line mixed their unease and worry over what else lie ahead of them. They wasted another day and left with no information.

Ch 23- Wilbur's truth

After spending several long days combing through the dusty shelves of the library, searching for any reference or clue related to the elusive ancient ritual, they finally decided to give up.

Their frustration mounted as they realized that despite their efforts, they had found nothing of significance.

The following day, when they returned to school, they were met with the wrath of Professor Erin. He was furious at their absence, having noticed that they had skipped school for several consecutive days without any explanation.

His disappointment was palpable as he scolded them for neglecting their studies and responsibilities. The tension in the classroom was thick, and the students exchanged worried glances, knowing they had let their curiosity lead them astray.

Professor Erin reminded them that while exploring the unknown was important, they must balance it with their academic obligations. As they listened to her lecture, they couldn't help but feel a mix of guilt and regret, wishing they had found a way to pursue their interests without neglecting their schoolwork.

That night, their desk was littered with a soul-crushing amount of homework paperwork. Emmanual and Louis started paying attention to the clock, and realized their time was almost up.

Turns out they needed to survive the night to finish off more than just the homework. They started piling their textbooks and papers up on top of each other.

The air became unfathomably tense, and the desk lamp illuminated just enough to see their focused faces took on the shadows of fatigue. The dim light revealed the glow of determination in their eyes.

Emmanual and Louis began working through the assignments, focusing on assignments one by one, occasionally stopping to share a quick joke, and give each other encouragement. Coffee cups began to pile up.

Between them was some fuel of caffeine just to stay awake and keep each other cooking; like Olympic athletes in training for an event, the next best thing, good grades. Despite fatigue, they put in the work to kill the average night while being focused on the oncoming dawn and workload; they were not going to let the work beat them out of their opportunity, no matter how late it got.

The following day, they stepped into school, tired and exhausted, having stayed up all night on too much coffee. They should have been grumpy, but the caffeine gave them an unexpected boost of energy.

Despite being tired, they were feeling awake because of the two or three cups of coffee and caffeine-laden energy drinks they had consumed throughout night.

Through the chaos of each hallway, they bounced off with the high from all of their caffeine, they felt alive and had an upper hand at least for that moment. They made more jokes and interactions with friends who were exhausted too from the previous night.

However, while they were relishing in they the high thro Min-Ality of caffeine, deep down they were slightly aware that drinking all that caffeine to try to keep going probably was not the least bit healthy.

They also knew they could not rely on the caffeine to last them throughout the day. However, for now the thrill of being able to stay awake and pay attention in their classes while being tired was so exhilarating.

When they moved on to first period, they were still hungry for excitement and came down enough to pay attention to the teacher, even if it was a struggle to keep their eyes open. It was a delicate balance between the highs of caffeine and the inevitable crash that awaited them later.

On that day after school, Louis and Emmanual were probably both feeling especially weary after a long day of class and activities.

The sun was beginning to set and it cast a warm glow on the trees and plants. The evening would have been beautiful if they were not so tired. As they walked along a path that they had travelled a thousand times before, they chatted about nothing in particular and laughed at the silliness of it all.

At a distance, they suddenly noticed a figure that seemed out of place. They both simultaneously noticed it too late to completely see it.

The figure was cloaked in shadow, and Louis and Emmanual were both so tired, that they were not able to fully perceive it.
At first, they both stopped and stared curiously, and then after they collected their thoughts, the weariness they were feeling began to influence what they thought they had just seen.

"It was probably just our imaginations," Louis said, while rubbing his eyes in a futile attempt to wipe the weariness away. Emmanual nodded, feeling relieved that they were both able to dismiss the unusual sight as just seeing something.

They decided to keep walking, dismissing the figure as a product of their hallucinations. They had no idea that what they had seen would be lingering in their minds, going from confusion to curiosity, and then to curiosity about the unknown, in the weeks to come.

With each day came a new kind of sadness and torment. They found themselves remembering happy times, and how laughter filled their home, and how now it was only silence.

They often found themselves coming together, and spending time with each other, yet his absence was always there even though they were together.

If one person started to talk about Cifer, they would all follow suit, more methodically trying to analyse his life and what final thoughts went into that decision. The questions plagued their minds and made moving on difficult.

A few days later, it seemed for Emmanuel that it going to be just another normal day, which consisted of class, lunch with friends, and perhaps some friendly jokes between lessons. But, that day would take a turn in the unexpected direction.

On that day, his close friend Louis was sick and wasn't attending school. His absence made the day seem dull and lonely as Emmanuel walked through the school halls and sat in classes alone, without Louis's company.

He missed the jokes and conversations they had. While he ate lunch, he felt the loneliness pervasive and an even stronger tinge of everyday malaise.

Without anyone to pick his thoughts from and without anyone to engage in discussions with, he felt like a ship with no sails lost at sea, wishing for Louis the familiar anchor of their friendship.

Emmanual returned home so worn down today; he was aching all over from a long day, and he was full of thoughts about his friend Louis. Little did he know how much he was missing Louis.

Without Louis around to lighten the mood, the day felt so uneventful and monotonous. He sat down on the edge of the bed and thought about how much he wanted to see if Louis was doing okay and if he was better and could enjoy his day.

He also wondered if he was depressed or bored without all the antics they usually did to add colour to their day.

It was a completely dull day for Emmanual at school, and it was torture listening to a bunch of the same boring lectures and listening to the drone of an empty classroom without Louis's laughter.

Emmanual decided that he needed to see his friend to fix both their days, and that was all the justification he needed to go meet Louis and make sure he was okay. He thought that it teased him to bring a bit of colour back into his friend.

As he was walking back home, the bright white figure appeared in front of him again and literally stopped him walking right into it.

The figure was now brighter than he remembered - "so bright" that it almost did not even seem to be on the ground anymore but rather hovering somehow! A wave of awe and confusion washed over him.

Just days prior he had convinced himself that the last experience was simply an illusion, smoke and mirrors, or maybe he was just exhausted.

Now he was standing in front of that figure again! It felt like the figure, somehow, was vibrating gently with some kind of energy and he felt drawn to it, literally begging him to come any closer.

Then he was thinking deep in thought about the consequences of seeing something so unbelievable. "Is it a message from the other side? a guardian? a figment of my mind?"

The air felt charged with some indescribable energy about it and somehow he realized it meant something, something he was supposed to figure out.

The mysterious shape attracted him, so alluring, that he swayed under its spell, tantalized by the bright white light that was radiating from it.

It was as if an invisible hand was touching him softly, beckoning him in closer to this shape. The light emanating from the shape seemed luminous; he wanted so desperately to feel the power of the light surrounding him.

The light was calling to him, the wonder of it all filled him with an ever-higher level of curiosity. More than with every step closer he took, it felt unearthly, drawing him closer and deeper into its embrace.

This irresistible force compelled him deeper and deeper into what was promising warmth and safety, and the anticipation of what was just on the other side rumbled in his spirit.

He went even closer to the white light, drawn in by its radiant glow and an inexplicable sense of curiosity.

The brilliance intensified, wrapping around him like a warm embrace, and before he knew it, he lost consciousness, his surroundings fading into oblivion.

When he finally awoke, he found himself in a place that was completely different from where he had been just moments before.

The air was filled with a peculiar fragrance, a mix of floral notes and something earthy, invigorating his senses.

As he opened his eyes, he realized he was lying on a soft, lush carpet of grass, illuminated by a gentle, golden sunlight that seemed to filter through the leaves of towering trees surrounding him.

The sky above was a brilliant shade of blue, dotted with fluffy white clouds that drifted lazily by. Confusion washed over him as he tried to comprehend how he had arrived in this strange, enchanting realm.

He was staggered and awed by the sight of the place, his heart racing to catch up to the dazzling view before him.

That place was completely enthralling; he felt like he had stepped into an entirely different dimension.

The colours sprang vibrantly all around him, luminous emerald green and jewelled sapphire blue blended into glorious rays of sunlight filtering down through the massive trees.

The strange sounds echoed all around him like whispers from another dimension, and the sweet scent of blooming flowers wrapped around him with tenderness.

He admired the strange plant and animal life, and every time he turned another piece of flora or faun was even more intriguing. It felt like an innocent, naive time filled with nature, where everything was laid back and harmonious, and laser-focused curiosity stirred in him to know all the secrets of the place.

He wanted to explore every inch and angle of the beauty and richness of the place and know the stories of it all.

He went further and was greeted by a white figure not as bright as the one he saw back then, the figure was stunningly beautiful, and Emmanual noticed it the moment he saw him.

Not only was his shape dazzling, but he also had a graceful, enchanting way about him that left Emmanual spellbound.

His movements were not just fluid and elegant, they created an atmosphere of beauty and inspiration. It was as if they separated him from the rest of beauty. It was unmistakable and left no one any room to look away from him.

The soft, pure light that shed on his condition was comparable to that of the morning star as dawn approaches; the faint light hinting at a quality of light that gave him an ethereal quality.

It was not sharp, or blinding, but more warm, golden, and fascinating. It suggested coziness and sympathy as if those drawn to him, wanted to come closer to the glow, and be warmed from it. He was quite something – every part of him was evenly developed; from his, deep-set eyes; perfectly shaped nose to his easy mouth (expressive) to his strong jaw - he had all parts standing in harmony with each measurement; quite interestingly easy to look at; so easy in fact, that we would wonder how long we had been staring.

Similarly, his hair shining a hugely striking silver appeared to be enchanted with its own living light; long and flowing - at times reaching down to the shoulders of his frame/gender - and naturally waving down his shoulders and would flow without second thought like a soft river down a mountain.

The way it captured the light – through angles - hinted that it had no normal given life span, exaggeratedly it gave it an unworldly unrealistic act.

He was carrying a gentle confident and calm expression that lent itself to too some sensibility of serenity for all that came into his space - so others at their darkest most complicated times - felt at ease; as one would; the attractiveness of wisdom mingled with kindness; more than the measure to age.

One walked into his space to experience an uncomfortably comfortable feeling, always grateful that they would be in the presence of joyful potential in a broken messy world.

Emmanual asked in awe "who are you?" the figure replied "I am Lucifer, I am a high-ranking archangel, right now you are in the realm of the Gods, God has summoned you to tell you something, and by the way, you are the first human here."

Lucifer leads Emmanual through the magnificent gates of God's palace, a grand structure that radiates light and an aura of divine authority.

As they step inside, Emmanual is awestruck by the breathtaking beauty that surrounds him—golden columns, shimmering light, and an ethereal atmosphere that seems to pulsate with life.

The place overflowed with pure Eather, it was magnificent. Emmanual could not believe what he was seeing.

Finally, they arrive before God, who sits upon a majestic throne, radiating a warmth that is both inviting and intimidating. Lucifer, with a sly smile, presents Emmanual, saying, "Behold, the human I have brought before you." God gazes down at Emmanual, a glimmer of recognition flashing in His eyes. "Hmm, looks like the one I was looking for," He replies thoughtfully.

Emmanual, still trying to comprehend the gravity of the situation, stammers, "Huh? You were looking for an idiot human like me?" The words escape his lips, revealing a mix of disbelief and self-deprecation, as he grapples with the idea that he could hold any significance in the grand scheme of the universe.

Emmanuel gazed around in confusion, attempting to process the bizarre scenario he found himself in. The strange glow surrounding him swirled with supernatural intensity, and the overwhelming strength and wisdom that came from the presence of God was almost blinding. "Why did you bring me to this world?" he stammered.

God, with a calm and peaceful demeanour said, "You were to be my successor." Emmanuel's mind was racing; he struggled to come to terms with the enormity of what he just heard. He blinked in disbelief.

"Me? Seriously? No way!" He could hardly contain himself as he contemplated the meaning of those words.

Emmanuel had never considered himself anything other than ordinary; he would never claim to have any extraordinary skills or divine qualities.

The idea of having any links to such a grand figure as a successor was surreal. "But I'm just me", he mumbled as he tried to make sense what was happening to him.

The prospect of Destiny filled the air, and he began searching for what lay ahead for him. What was meant by successor to God?

"Yep, you're one of my potential successors." Emmanuel stares blankly at God, then leans back in his chair, shaking his head in disbelief. "ONE of your potential successors?" he asks, confused. "What does it mean, 'One'? How many do you have?" Emmanuel suddenly can't seem to shake this crazy whirlwind of thoughts and emotions.

He struggles to fathom what he could bring to the table in order to be of any significance. The thought of a successor - your successor - is exhilarating and terrifying.

Just for the hell of it, he enthusiastically considers all of the responsibilities, stress, liability, and hope this comes with. "Are there others like me?" he wonders. "And what does it mean to get picked? What are you looking for in us?" The conversation has left Emmanuel very much confused yet curious about the possibilities...

God gently chided Emmanuel, "My child while your given desire and curiosity are justified, I urge you to take a little more patience. You will find out the truth about your successor and who will ultimately take that position, at the ceremony this evening. You will have answers to all of your questions, and will know all the mystery behind this subject. So, for now. Hold your horses until this event, and know that it will happen in due time. Remember, the tussle you have gone through and the anticipation leading up to the reveal of whatever it is can sometimes outweigh the actual reveal itself. So, step back, calm your heart, and prepare. The ceremony this evening will help you understand and I promise it will be worth the wait! You will be glad you took this time prior to that ceremony. Your delay will eventually pay off just believe that you will see how everything fits into my plan."

Lucifer then escorts Emmanual back to the realm from which he initially came. As they traverse the ethereal pathways, Emmanual's eyes are drawn to shimmering lights in the distance. To his astonishment, he sees the radiant soul of none other than Akira Toriyama, the legendary mangaka renowned for creating iconic characters and stories that have shaped the world of anime and manga.

Emmanual feels a wave of reverence wash over him as he recalls the profound impact Toriyama's work has had on countless fans across generations.

Continuing along their journey, Emmanual spots another familiar soul—Seth Bling, celebrated as the greatest Redstone user in the vast universe of Minecraft. Intrigued, he approaches Seth, eager to engage in conversation.

The two exchange pleasantries, and Emmanual, filled with curiosity, inquiries about the whereabouts of the famed Minecraft legend, Technoblade. With a confident smile, Seth replies, "He is not dead; Technoblade never dies."

This statement fills Emmanual with hope, as it resonates deeply with the spirit of resilience and creativity that defines the Minecraft community.

Author's note

Thank you so much for reading ***the eyes of the wicked***: *Volume 1*. Writing this book has been an incredible journey, and I'm beyond grateful that you chose to step into this world with me.

Emmanual's story is far from over. The powers he's discovered, the mysteries he's uncovered, and the enemies he's yet to face are only the beginning. There are still many secrets hidden within the world of Eather, and much more to explore in the realms beyond.

I'm currently working on *Volume 2*, and I promise it'll be even more intense, emotional, and action-packed. You'll get to dive deeper into the history of the eyes, learn more about the legendary swords, and witness Emmanual face challenges that will test not just his strength — but his heart.

Stay tuned.
And again — thank you for reading.

-   Arhaan jiwani and Karthikeya Varma